## TESTING THE WATERS

Kevin burped, then giggled as a thought occurred to him. "I guess I'm the master of the universe."

"Ah, put a leash on it!" said Josh.

"No way." Kevin's imagination had been strapped to a post long enough. He stood up, hungry for something more than fast food, and climbed on a high boulder, reaching a hand up to the heavens.

Josh laughed. "Whatcha gonna do? Part the Red Sea?"

"Something like that."

Josh stopped laughing and watched as Kevin stared through his glasses at the infinite depths of the star-filled sky.

"Clouds," he whispered to the night. The frame of the glasses began to get warm, the lenses went dark and then silver. Directly above them, a gray spot appeared, like a hole in the sky, and clouds began to unfold, growing high above their heads—dense gray clouds, but the glasses reflected them in rich, swirling hues.

"Pretty intense," said Josh. "Now stop it."

## ALSO BY NEAL SHUSTERMAN

*Downsiders*

*Speeding Bullet*

*Full Tilt*

Visit the author at **www.storyman.com**

# The Eyes of
# KID MIDAS
## NEAL SHUSTERMAN

**SIMON PULSE**
**NEW YORK LONDON TORONTO SYDNEY**

First Simon Pulse edition September 2004

Text copyright © 1992 by Neal Shusterman

SIMON PULSE
An imprint of Simon & Schuster
Children's Publishing Division
1230 Avenue of the Americas
New York, NY 10020

SIMON PULSE and colophon are registered trademarks of
Simon & Schuster, Inc.

Printed in the United States of America
10 9 8 7 6 5 4 3 2 1

Library of Congress Cataloging-in-Publication Data
Shusterman, Neal.
The eyes of Kid Midas / Neal Shusterman.—1st Simon Pulse ed.
p. cm.
Summary: Kevin is entranced when he finds a pair of sunglasses
that turn his desires into reality, but then things start to get out of
control.
ISBN 0-689-87349-2 (pbk.)
[1. Magic—Fiction. 2. Eyeglasses—Fiction.] I. Title.
PZ7.S55987Ey       2004
[Fic]—dc22             2004000401

for Jarrod,
in whose eyes
I can see infinity

# Acknowledgments

*The Eyes of Kid Midas* has evolved over a period of ten years from a campfire tale to this novel, and there are many people who have had a hand in shaping it.

A very special thanks to all the kids who have heard the many incarnations of the story: Jeff, Jonas, Jason, Seth, and everyone at Camp Anawana; Tracy and all the kids at The Farm School; everyone at Phoenix Recreation; Vicki Croskrey and her students at Vista Verde School.

Thanks to Steph, who had faith that I would eventually get it right; Lloyd, who midwifed Kid Midas's prolonged labor; Clinnette (C.J.), without whom it could never have been finished; and Elaine, without whose constant love and support Kevin Midas would never have crossed the threshold from dream to reality.

With people like these, who needs magic glasses?

# THE EYES OF KID MIDAS

# CHAPTER 1

# Four-eyes Midas Eats a Pinecone

When Kevin Midas first saw the mountain, it was in perfect focus, because his glasses were not yet broken. The peak stood alone, like a single stone tooth that had been thrust up from deep within the earth, somewhere near the beginning of time. It wasn't part of a larger range; it didn't fit in with the rolling hills around it, it was just simply there, defying all attempts to explain it.

The vans approached from the west, giving all the kids on the camping trip the most dramatic view the mountain offered. Its western face was a sheer wall of stone that towered hundreds of feet into the air. The eastern side was a much smoother slope, covered with pines—the same pines that blanketed the foothills around them. It was only half a mountain, really—as if someone had sliced it down the middle, leaving a granite cliff to face forever west.

"Wow!" was all Kevin could say when he saw

it. Even Josh looked up to stare at it. Josh, who was Kevin's most consistent friend, sat next to him for the entire three-hour trip, playing an endless supply of pocket video games. The sight of the mountain was the only thing that could take Josh away from his games.

"There it is," said Mr. Kirkpatrick, the teacher driving their van, "the Divine Watch!"

They pulled into a picture spot with the other three vans, and everyone got out to admire the magnificent peak before them. From photos, Kevin knew that the Divine Watch came to a sharp peak, but right now the top of the mountain shrouded in clouds. Even so, it was more impressive than pictures could ever show. No wonder the Indians had built legends around it.

Most of the twenty kids on the camping trip had cameras, which now began to snap away like crazy.

Bertram Tarson, who, thankfully, had not been in the same van with Kevin and Josh, watched the photo frenzy and rolled those golf-ball eyes of his.

"For God's sake, it's only a stupid mountain," grumbled Bertram from behind a huge wad of bubble gum that Kevin could smell twenty feet away.

Kevin couldn't say he hated Bertram Tarson, because hate was too mild a word for what Kevin felt. Bertram was more than a mere bully—he was a constant reminder that Kevin's life was out of his control. At home Kevin's parents controlled every waking moment, and in school control fell into the hands of the tough kids like Bertram, who, only three weeks into the seventh grade, had already resumed the endless pecking that kept Kevin angry and humiliated most of the time. Kevin wondered why nature pulled the cruel trick of making all the really obnoxious kids grow so much faster than the others. So much faster than him.

As the shortest kid in the grade, with the thickest glasses, control of his own destiny seemed about as far from Kevin as a slam dunk on a basketball court. Bertram was proof of that.

"Don't look now," whispered Josh, "but Bertram's staring at you." Josh, who was black, had no love for kids like Bertram, who saw everyone else in the world as potential targets for hatred.

The fact that Bertram was glaring at Kevin was not a good sign. Everyone knew that Bertram needed a daily fix of cruelty, and he would often stare at his prey in advance, concocting some scheme.

Bertram kept his eyes focused on Kevin for the longest time as he chomped up and down on his Big-League Chew with teeth so crooked they would make a horse cry. Bertram had worn braces for as long as Kevin could remember, but he suspected the braces would lose the battle.

"What are you looking at, *Shrimpoid*?" Bertram finally said to Kevin. Then he reached into his mouth and pulled out a gum wad the size of his fist, depositing it into the waiting hand of Hal Hornbeck, a hulking kid who was Bertram's second-in-command. Hal was every bit as mean as Bertram, only less intelligent—which really didn't mean much. It was like calling a potato less intelligent than an onion.

Bertram strolled back into his van, and Hal, who had been taking scowling lessons from Bertram, scowled at Kevin as he rolled Bertram's gum into a ball. He flung the ball at Kevin, but the gum missed the mark entirely, lodging itself in Mr. Kirkpatrick's hair. The gum clung to the hair almost as well as it clung to Bertram's dental work.

Mr. Kirkpatrick turned to see Hal Hornbeck lumber into the van. Kirkpatrick just sighed. "All right, everyone," he said, "back in the vans; the Divine Watch awaits."

*Awaits what?* wondered Kevin—because, through Kevin Midas's glasses, the lonely mountain cloaked in morning mist did seem to be waiting.

The mountain loomed closer and closer in the windshield until all that could be seen was the immense rock wall.

When the van door rolled open, Kevin was the first one out.

The curtain of clouds had lifted to reveal the peak; a sharp point piercing the sky. Kevin, who at thirteen was rarely impressed by anything, was so overwhelmed, he had to lean back against the van for balance.

Bertram was also the first one out of his van—but for reasons other than sight-seeing.

Kevin's crystal-clear image of the mountain suddenly became a shadowy blur as Bertram ripped the glasses from Kevin's face.

"The ball is in play!" shouted Bertram, who, after three hours of being cooped up in a van, needed a victim. No doubt he had been looking forward to this for hours.

With his blasting boom box in one hand and Kevin's glasses in the other, Bertram ran to the edge of the trees with Hal, and they stood there gloating and leering—waiting for Kevin to chase them.

"Don't do it, Kevin," said Josh, who had seen the whole thing. "If you stop chasing them, they'll stop doing it."

Sound advice, but the urge to go after them was so strong, Kevin didn't know if he could resist.

He turned to see the teachers too busy with the head count to notice Kevin's plight. (Apparently Ian Axelrod was nowhere to be found. Ralphy Sherman swore he had succumbed to spontaneous human combustion somewhere along the interstate, but then, Ralphy said that whenever someone couldn't be found.)

Bertram leered at Kevin with those awful bulging eyes as he spun the glasses on his index finger.

"Bertram's like a zit," said Josh. "Ignore it and it will eventually go away."

But Kevin simply couldn't do that. The ball was in play, and it seemed Kevin Midas was eternally condemned to play other kids' ball games.

Already fuming mad, Kevin raced toward Bertram, and Bertram took off with Hal through the trees, leaving a trail of heavy metal for Kevin to follow.

Kevin burst into a clearing filled with dead grass surrounding an evil-looking outhouse. Hal came from behind and put Kevin into the infamous Hornbeck Extremely Full Nelson (which was just like a normal full nelson, only more so).

Kevin kicked and struggled against Hal, and the sport turned from a ball game to a rodeo.

"Jest looga that dowgie go!" said Hal, putting on a fake Texas accent. "How fast you think we can rope this dowgie, Bertram?"

Kevin had a fleeting image of himself with his arms and legs looped together like a calf in a rodeo, and being left there for the rest of the day.

Hal took the edge off the nelson just enough for Kevin to see Bertram, standing ten feet away. A steady beat pounded from Bertram's tape player, which now rested on the ground, as Bertram dangled Kevin's glasses from his fingers. The game was no longer a rodeo, but a bullfight.

"C'mon, Midas. Come an' get your glasses!" said Bertram. *"Toro, toro!"*

Hal cackled with laughter. Kevin, barely able to breathe, could only grunt and snort like a bull.

Josh lurched into the clearing and, as was often the case, immediately took up Kevin's cause. His parents were lawyers, and so Josh had a way of talking sense and logic into onions and potatoes.

"You realize, Bertram," said Josh, "that you're already in enough trouble for the gum in Kirkpatrick's hair. If I were you, I'd lay low for a while."

Kevin could almost hear the advice go in one ear, echo a bit, then come out of the other.

"Hal threw it," said Bertram.

"It was *your* gum," said Josh.

Bertram shrugged it off and returned his attention to the bullfight. Then Bertram's music, which had been blaring all the years Kevin knew him, suddenly stopped dead.

Kevin could hear the rush of a distant waterfall and birds singing high up in the pine trees—sounds of nature that must have infuriated Bertram.

"Huh?" said Bertram, turning around. Josh ejected the tape and backed away with it. Kevin's eyes went wide. No one who valued his life turned off Bertram's music. Bertram gritted his thoroughbred teeth, and growled like a hungry pit bull.

"You had best give me back that tape!"

Josh continued to back away with the hostage cassette, heading toward the outhouse.

The small green outhouse was the size of a phone booth, and it had one of those odors you re-

member for the rest of your life. Josh swung open
the door and an unholy strangling stench flowed
out like invisible fingers of death.

Bertram started toward him, but Josh held the
tape out over the open hole of the grungy toilet.

"Take one more step, and down it goes."

Kevin, still in the crushing grip of the Extremely
Full Nelson, watched as Josh Wilson rendered Bertram Tarson speechless. It was a moment for the
record books.

"C'mon, Josh, a joke's a joke," pleaded Bertram. "You wouldn't do that . . . would you?"

Josh smiled. "Make you a deal. I'll give you
back your music if you let Kevin go and give him
back his glasses."

Bertram didn't answer right away.

"The offer is good for five seconds," said Josh.

Bertram turned to Hal and nodded. Hal threw
Kevin to the ground, and Kevin gasped a deep
breath.

"Good," said Josh. "Now the glasses."

"The tape first."

"You have three seconds," said Josh.

Powerless to bargain, Bertram tossed the glasses
to Kevin. Josh then tossed Bertram his tape, keeping his part of the deal—which, under the circumstances, was not the safest thing to do.

"Josh, look out!" yelled Kevin, but it was too
late. Bertram grabbed Josh by the neck and

smashed his back against the wall of the outhouse with a thud, pinning him there.

"You touched my tunes," screamed Bertram, his face turning red. "Nobody touches my tunes!" Hal held open the outhouse door, and in one instant the plan became painfully clear. Bertram and Hal began to pull Josh headfirst toward the outhouse.

"Listen," reasoned Josh, "you really don't want to do this. . . . Think of your conscience!"

"I ain't got one," said Bertram.

That's when Kevin threw the pinecone. It whizzed through the air and bounced off the back of Bertram's head.

Bertram slowly turned to Kevin, who stood across the clearing with the determination of a gunslinger. Kevin had taken enough. He could sense something igniting inside himself—something that was about to explode.

"Oh my God!" said Josh—realizing that Kevin meant business.

Bertram offered up a sinister smile at Kevin's foolhardy attempt at bravery. "*You* threw a pinecone at *me*, Midas?"

Kevin, unflinching, pushed the glasses farther up on his face, and two words growled themselves out from the back of his throat.

"Your mother."

Bertram's smile faded. The only thing more sacred than Bertram's music was his mother. He dropped Josh, forgetting him completely, and stared at Kevin, fists clenched. His face was popping blood vessels, and his whole body quivered in fury.

"My mother what?"

Kevin clenched his own fists and readied himself for the fight. He stared straight at Bertram from across the clearing and shot his words from the hip.

"Your *mother's* a pinecone."

A hundred yards away, at the campsight, Miss Argus, the math teacher, was lovingly snipping gum out of Mr. Kirkpatrick's hair. So involved were they in their minor surgical procedure that neither they nor the other teachers observing the operation noticed when Ian Axelrod, finally turning up, came bounding from the woods and announced, "Hey, everyone, Bertram's fighting Kevin Midas!"

In a matter of seconds all twenty kids had vanished from the campsight, racing through the woods to see the fight of the century.

Kevin and Bertram rolled in the dirt, both delivering punch after punch. In seconds they were surrounded by a cheering mass of kids who were thrilled that somebody—anybody—was going to get beaten up. Josh tried to break it up, but Hal put him in an Extremely Full Nelson.

Kevin had exploded, all right—he was a fireball

of fury, finding more strength in himself than he'd ever known he had. At last he had discovered the courage to stand up to Bertram! At last, after all these years, Bertram would get what he deserved: humiliation at the hands of Kevin Midas.

But as it sometimes goes, Kevin's fury just wasn't enough. Bertram was simply bigger and stronger—and all the righteous rage in the world wasn't going to change that.

In the end, Bertram pinned Kevin down by the neck with one hand and brandished the pinecone in the other, holding it above Kevin's mouth.

"Open wide, Mid*ass*," said Bertram.

"Go to hell, Bertram!" yelled Kevin defiantly, and with that, Bertram rammed the entire pinecone into Kevin's mouth, until Kevin's cheeks bulged like a chipmunk's.

Bertram got off Kevin, and stepped back to admire his handiwork.

Then everyone but Josh began to laugh at Kevin—even Nicole Patterson, the girl whom Kevin had a not-so-secret crush on. The humiliation hurt worse than his black eye and swelling mouth.

"Hey," said some clown, "Kevin's eating a high-fiber diet!" More laughter.

Kevin reached into his mouth and carefully dislodged the pinecone.

The crowd started to thin, but Bertram still stood there like a proud hunter over his kill. Just beside

Bertram were Kevin's glasses, which had fallen during the fight. Without taking his eyes off Kevin, Bertram lifted his foot and very slowly brought his dirty Reebok down on the glasses, grinding them into the dusty ground with all of his weight until the glasses snapped.

"Oops," said Bertram. He lifted his foot from the broken glasses, grabbed his tape player, and left the clearing, his victory now complete.

Three weeks into the new school year, and his glasses were already destroyed.

"He's gonna pay for this," mumbled Kevin, fighting back tears. "He's gonna pay."

Josh just shook his head as he helped Kevin up. "Somebody's got to do something about him," said Josh. "The psycho's totally out of control."

As they left, Kevin turned to look up at the mountain, which was nothing but a big blur now. *"He's gonna pay,"* Kevin would always say when Bertram laid into him, but lately Kevin wasn't sure that Bertram would ever pay for anything. He wondered if the world was really a place where all the Bertrams and Hals were somehow brought to justice—or if it was like the mountain, which merely watched in silence as Kevin was beaten to a pulp.

# CHAPTER 2

# *The Divine Watch*

Kevin didn't think of climbing the mountain until much later that night. The idea first occurred to him sometime around twilight, but he pushed it away. There were more pressing things to think about. Like how was he going to face the world looking the way he did?

It was sunset now, and the white cliff of the mountain had taken on a bright red face, bathing the campsite in unearthly shades of scarlet and vermilion. Most of the other kids were clustered around the campfire, making s'mores, but Kevin wasn't about to leave his tent.

His small travel mirror showed him an eye as bruised as they come and lips puffy and swollen from the painful kiss of the pinecone. He barely recognized himself.

Bertram had, of course, received a reprimand from Kirkpatrick and was "put on warning"—the same warning he had lived under his entire life. He had no problems facing the world with a reprimand.

But for Kevin to go out now, with the evidence of Bertram's victory all over his face—that he couldn't do. So instead he just stayed inside, peering out of the slit of his open tent like a hermit.

It was Josh who dragged him out.

"If you don't come out," said Josh, "it'll make Bertram look even better. It'll mean he beat you up so bad you were ashamed to show your face."

Kevin had to accept the logic, as much as he hated to.

The sun was already beneath the horizon when Kevin shuffled over to the campfire. Now the mountain reflected a rich purple blanket across the campsite that clashed with the flickering orange flames of the fire.

Kevin couldn't quite make out the faces, but he imagined that they all stared at him as he sat down.

He grabbed a marshmallow stick and poked it into the fire, sending sparks that flew into the air and faded quickly out of focus. Embarrassed to look up, Kevin just listened as Kirkpatrick rambled on in his earth-science sort of way about the mountain.

"The Divine Watch," he said, "is a mountain of mystery, a place with roots dating back thousands of years." Kirkpatrick turned to look at the dark peak, its shade of violet getting deeper and deeper. "It was sacred to the Native Americans. They called it 'The Eye of God.' "

Now Kevin began to pay attention. When he squinted, he could make out Kirkpatrick's face across the fire. He was leaning into the center of the circle, drawing everyone into the story.

"The Native Americans believed that the sun-god peered off the top of the mountain each morning to drive back the forces of darkness and clear a path for the coming day. They feared that if he slept through dawn and didn't fight back the darkness, the sun would never rise again, and the world would be thrown into chaos."

Kevin reached into his pocket and pulled out a badly scratched eyeglass lens. He peered through it at the mountain. Its face was completely black now—an absolute ebony against a sky filling with stars.

Kevin began to forget his swollen mouth and black eye as he listened to Mr. Kirkpatrick weave the ancient legend.

"There's a prophecy," said Mr. Kirkpatrick, "that goes something like this:"

The flames began to leap higher as he spoke.

> *In the balance of dark and day,*
> *The endless battle; the lasting peace,*
> *Our lives are born of the dying dream,*
> *In the balance of dark and day.*

"What does it mean?" someone asked.

"It *means*," said Nicole Patterson, who always

knew what everything *meant*, "that if morning never came, we would sleep forever and never wake up."

"Something like that," said Mr. Kirkpatrick, raising his eyebrows.

Bertram tossed a plastic fork into the fire.

"Dumb Indians," said Bertram. "What do they know?" The plastic fork twisted to a slow, painful end in the flames.

"I think they knew quite a lot, Bertram," said Mr. Kirkpatrick, "because that's not where the story ends." The last glow of twilight was gone from the sky now, and the fire played on Mr. Kirkpatrick's face. That and his crazy gum-shorn hair made him look like a shaman—an Indian medicine man.

"There's another place," he said, "fifty miles to the west, called the Devil's Punch Bowl. It's a huge bowl a mile wide, carved into the stone like the crater of a meteor, and in the very center of the bowl is a tall spike of rock, hundreds of feet high. That spike is called the Devil's Chair."

"So?" said Hal.

"So," said Mr. Kirkpatrick, "about a hundred years ago, two astronomers discovered something incredible! They discovered that the shadow of the very tip of the Divine Watch rests on the Devil's Chair at dawn, twice a year!"

"When?" asked Josh.

"I know!" Kevin blurted out. " 'In the balance

of dark and day.' That must be the spring and fall equinox—it's the only time when both the day and night are exactly twelve hours long!"

Mr. Kirkpatrick gave a broad shaman's smile.

Josh smiled back at him, calling his bluff. "How conveeeeenient," said Josh, "that tomorrow is September twenty-first—the fall equinox. C'mon, Mr. Kirkpatrick—the whole thing's a bunch of baloney, isn't it?"

"Yeah," Bertram agreed, greatly relieved. "I knew it. I knew it all along."

"Maybe," said Mr. Kirkpatrick. "And maybe not." With that, he got up from the circle and poured a bucket of water on the flames. "Pleasant dreams," he said as the steamy smoke rose to meet the heavens.

The moon peeked its full, round face from behind the Divine Watch, casting a pitch-black shadow of the mountain across the forest.

There were more stars in the sky than Kevin had ever seen before. Enough to make the sky seem impossibly deep, and the universe impossibly large. Kevin had done a comprehensive ten-page report on the universe last year. There were supernovas and giant quasars out there at the far reaches of existence. There were billions of stars in each galaxy, and there were more galaxies than people on the face of the earth. Just thinking about it could make a person realize how small and insignificant his own problems were.

But not Kevin.

"Are you coming in, or what?" asked Josh. He had already satisfied his interest in the majesty of nature and was now in the small tent they shared, reading a comic book. The tent was gradually filling with mosquitoes and moths that flew in holding patterns around Josh's flashlight. Kevin, who stood just outside the tent, had left the zipper on the mosquito net open.

Kevin couldn't turn away from the mountain because he had the uncanny feeling that it was watching him. A soft wind rasped through the trees, and Kevin imagined if a mountain was a living thing—if it could breathe—this is what it would sound like.

*"Put a leash on that imagination,"* his mother's voice said in his head, *"before it drags you across the lawn."*

Kevin broke his trance and stepped into the tent.

"Listen to this," said Josh, flipping a page in his comic book. "The Steroid Avenger gets sucked into a black hole, travels back forty years in time, and accidentally kills his father."

"Can't do it," said Kevin, "because then he'd never get born."

"That's the thing," said Josh. "Now the only way he can get born is if he *becomes* his own father."

"Gross!" said Kevin. "It means he has to marry his mother."

Josh shrugged. "That's what you get for messing with time and space."

Kevin zipped the mosquito netting closed. Considering the events of the day, Kevin idly wished *he* could be sucked into a black hole and end up in some other universe entirely. He slipped into his sleeping bag and stared up at the peak of the tent, wondering if the mountain could still see him through the thin blue vinyl.

As Kevin lay there, an idea began to boil in his mind, until he had to open his mouth and let it overflow.

"I'm gonna climb the mountain," said Kevin, not yet knowing how serious he really was.

"In your dreams," said Josh, returning to his comic book.

Kevin ought to have left it at that, but the thought nagged at him as much as the pain in his eye and mouth did. As much as the sounds in his head of kids laughing.

"I'm climbing it tonight," said Kevin, "and I don't care if I get in trouble. *I'll* be the one there at dawn—and I'll stand at the top, waving down to everyone. I'll even give Bertram the finger."

Josh turned his flashlight into Kevin's face, and Kevin squinted. "You're serious, aren't you?"

"You can come if you want," said Kevin.

Josh held the flashlight on Kevin's face a moment longer, and when Kevin didn't break out laughing, Josh turned off his light. The tent seemed much smaller in the dark, and their words seemed much more important.

"You think Mr. Kirkpatrick's story was real?" whispered Josh.

"I don't know. But there's only one way to find out; be there at dawn. In the balance of dark and day."

Josh took forever to think it through.

"Why do you want to do this?" he finally asked.

Kevin shrugged. "Because it's there," he said. But that wasn't it. "Because no one thinks we'd have the guts to do it," he added. But that was only part of it. The rest was something far bigger. It had to do with the way the mountain stared at him— the way it just wouldn't leave him alone. Its dark face had gravity that was pulling Kevin toward it.

"Because," said Kevin, "if there really is magic in this mountain, then *I* want to be the one to find it."

Kevin and Josh waited, fully dressed, in their dark tent, listening to the voices of the other kids as they settled down for the night. Then they listened to the teachers, who sat around complaining about the principal the way the kids complained about their teachers. Finally there were no voices—only the chorus of crickets and the rustling of leaves.

They began the trek sometime around midnight;

the very excitement of the climb propelled them through the quarter mile of woods to the great stone face of the Divine Watch.

"We'll have to walk around to the other side," said Kevin, "The eastern slope should be a cinch."

"This is nuts," sighed Josh. "Someone oughta reach in through your ears and slap that shrimpoid brain of yours."

The mountain breathed a chilling wind down the face of the cliff, and Josh looked up. Kevin could see concern building up in Josh's eyes. Josh wasn't the worrying type, but on the rare occasions when he *did* find something worth worrying about, he would worry himself silly.

"People die climbing mountains, Kevin," said Josh. "Bears bite their heads off, and vultures pick at their bones. I just thought you should know."

"I'm not turning back."

Josh zipped the last few teeth of his jacket zipper until he was as warm as he was going to get.

"Are you scared, Kevin?"

"I've never been so scared in my life," Kevin said with a smile. Kevin Midas never knew it could feel this great, being this scared.

# CHAPTER 3

# The Balance
# of Dark and Day

As anyone who has done it can tell you, most of
the really important mountain-climbing lessons are
learned the first time. Kevin's and Josh's first lessons were, in fact, five of the most important ones:

1. *Mountains are a heck of a lot larger than they
   look.*
2. *Granite is just as hard as you think it is.*
3. *Just because trees might be growing on a slope,
   that doesn't mean it ain't steep.*
4. *Flashlights are useless unless you've got a
   whole lot of batteries.*

All of this added together equals the biggest
lesson of all:

5. *Never, ever climb a mountain at night.*

None of this, however, was going to stop Kevin and Josh.

It took them over an hour to make their way around the face of the mountain and find a point where they could begin climbing. Another hour later, their flashlights could only create dull brown patches on the ground that wouldn't help an ant find its way.

Halfway through the night, lit only by the bright moonlight, Kevin and Josh were beginning to stumble. Their legs were getting scratched and bruised through their jeans, and the soles of their Nikes were fraying and going bald faster than Mr. Kirkpatrick.

And there was the ever-present sense that they were not alone on the mountain.

With nothing but forest sounds and the monotonous padding of his own aching feet to occupy his mind, Kevin's vivid imagination began to conjure up all sorts of dark mountain terrors. Bigfoot to the left, mountain lions to the right, and up ahead the fluttering of bats. Vampire bats. Big ones that could swarm over you and suck you dry in seconds, the way piranhas could devour a horse. *And vultures would pick at our bones,* thought Kevin.

Kevin knew Josh was thinking the same sorts of things, but he wasn't saying anything. As long as they didn't slow down and didn't talk about it, everything would be fine. The farther they got, the harder it was to turn back—especially with all those sounds echoing behind them.

After what seemed like an eternity, the trees became fewer and farther between, until they finally gave way to prickly bushes and jagged rocks. The moon was a pumpkin on the horizon, and dawn gently hinted on the opposite side of the sky. It was sometime around five-thirty when they finally dared to rest on a flat granite plateau.

Kevin looked up at the mountain summit as he dumped sand and pebble from his ruined shoes. It still appeared far away.

"I don't know who's dumber," said Josh, "you for coming up with this stupid idea, or me for coming with you!"

Kevin leaned back against the cold rock, trying to catch his breath. "We're almost there," he said. Now dawn was wasting no time. Kevin could already see a blurry ribbon of red where the sun would eventually rise.

"You know, I've been thinking," said Josh. "Maybe . . . maybe if something *does* happen up there at sunrise . . . maybe we're not supposed to see it."

"I thought you didn't believe the story," said Kevin.

"I don't," said Josh. "But still . . ."

Kevin imagined some of the things that might happen. Their hair could turn white. They could be blinded for life. At almost six in the morning, after a sleepless night, Kevin could believe almost anything.

"Naah," said Kevin. "Anyway, if we weren't supposed to be here, something would have stopped us by now."

"Killed us, you mean," corrected Josh.

That's when they heard it again—more clearly than before. The steady padding of feet, and a hint of heavy breath—like an animal—a huge animal on four feet. Kevin and Josh froze as they looked down the slope into darkness.

Kevin smelled it before they saw anything—a sickly sweet smell, like rotting fruit. Kevin instantly knew the nature of the beast by its smell.

"It's Bertram!" said Kevin.

And thirty-some-odd yards down the mountain came a distant, surprised voice. "Who's that?"

Kevin and Josh could see more clearly now—there were two of them. Hal and Bertram had dared to climb the mountain together, and now they stared at Kevin and Josh with jaws dropped halfway to their knees.

Bertram clenched his fists and gritted his donkey teeth. "Midas," he screamed, "if you and Wilson get to the top before we do, you die!"

That was all Kevin needed to hear.

"Let's go! Move your butt!" Kevin nearly dragged Josh up the mountain with him. This was *their* climb, and Kevin would rather die than let Bertram and Hal muscle in on it.

The top of the mountain, which had seemed so far away before, now looked close enough for Kevin to touch. It came to a sharp peak, like a witch's hat, but the very top was flat, and just big enough, perhaps, for someone to stand on it.

*That someone is going to be me!* thought Kevin as he lifted his aching feet one after the other, getting higher and higher.

There were no more bushes to grab on to, only sharp stone. "Dead meat!" yelled Bertram. "You guys are both dead meat!"

Kevin didn't care. Chills ran down the length of his body, and his fingertips began to tingle. He had actually climbed a mountain! Suddenly Kevin no longer felt exhausted, no longer felt the fear of the climb. All that remained in him was a burning desire to touch the top of the Watch. He reached down to help Josh, and Josh helped push Kevin higher when there wasn't anything to grip. They were a perfect team, and now Josh was filled with the same determination Kevin felt. Kevin almost had to fight to stay in the lead.

"If we do this, Kevin," said Josh, "we'll be legends. We'll be legends forever."

Bertram and Hal were closing in, right on Josh's tail. Screaming at each other, blaming each other for not moving fast enough.

The four boys found themselves clinging to the

mountain at the steepest part of the climb, and for the first time Kevin could see how high and dangerous this climb was; one slip and he would crash down onto hard rocks hundreds of feet below. The fear only added to his excitement. Wouldn't his parents just roll over and die if they saw him now? He would have laughed—if he could catch his breath.

The crimson horizon had bloomed into a bright blue streak of dawn, and the night raced away with a howling wind that tore at the boys as they scaled the last few feet of the Divine Watch. In moments the sun would peer over the horizon, marking the balance of dark and day. Bertram and Hal were in line right below Josh and had given up trying to get there first. Now they would settle for getting there, period. It was as if the rest of the world had vanished, and all that remained were four boys, and the brutally steep mountain.

The wind chilled Kevin to the bone, buffeting his exhausted body. It blew into his face, making his eyes wet and cold. Above him, the clouds changed shape and danced by faster than any Kevin had ever seen before.

He reached out his right hand, stretching it as far as he possibly could, and finally, after a whole night climbing, his fingertips touched the flat top of the Divine Watch. He reached up his left hand and pulled himself up so that he could gaze across the top.

As Kevin's eyes cleared the top of the Watch, the first rays of sun shot from the horizon behind him, growing more powerful with each passing moment. They hit his back, warming his ice-cold neck. The bright light cast the shadow of Kevin's curly blond head across the smooth tabletop surface of the Divine Watch. Yes—that's what it was like—a polished stone tabletop, smooth and round, no more than three feet across.

Even with his fuzzy vision, Kevin could tell that the view was spectacular. The mountains before him gave way to rolling hills and then an expanse of desert, still cloaked in shadow. Beyond the desert was a blur that could have been anything to his nearsighted eyes.

"What's it like, Kevin?" yelled Josh over the sound of the wind.

"Do you see anything up there?" yelled Hal.

Kevin looked at the smooth surface. There *was* something there! Something small and shiny; a ball of light grabbing the sun, changing its color and scattering it across the mountaintop, but the glare from the sun made it hard for Kevin to see what it was.

"Well, what's happening up there, Midas?" yelled Bertram. "We ain't got all day!"

Kevin squinted his eyes and pulled himself up another inch, until his head eclipsed the sun, and the object was trapped in his shadow. The object, which seemed so formless before, now had a definite shape that Kevin recognized immediately.

"It's . . . it's a pair of glasses!" said Kevin.

"Aw, you've got to be kidding!" cried Hal.

"No, really!" It was a pair of sunglasses, dark, sleek, and smooth. Its lenses were a single visor-like blade suspended from a black-and-gold half frame. The dark, silvery lenses seemed to shimmer with colors, like the northern lights.

*Someone must have been here before*, thought Kevin. *Instead of carving their initials, they must have left the glasses to stake their claim.*

As Kevin stretched out his arm across the Divine Watch, toward the glasses, the wind screamed in his ears, and the reality he'd been fighting back all night suddenly took hold.

What was he doing here? He could fall! He could die! What was he thinking? Panic screamed at him, like a thousand voices in the wind, demanding he leave this dangerous place now and get back to the campsite this very instant.

Still, he wanted those glasses. They would be his prize for reaching the top first. He fought against the panicking voices and hooked the glasses with his index finger, pulling them toward him.

"Let us get up there, Midas. Get out of the way!" demanded Bertram.

"Just a second." Kevin looked at the glasses closely. They were the height of style, and must have been very, very expensive. He put them on, hooking the smooth gold-and-black half frame around his ears.

Blackness . . .

. . . then a speck of light as his eyes began to adjust to the dark lenses. But it was more than just his eyes adjusting. It was as if the lenses were lightening up for his eyes, bringing everything into focus. These weren't mere sunglasses—they seemed to fit Kevin's prescription as well. They were perfect. All right—they were a bit too big for his head, but otherwise they couldn't be beat.

Now the view before him stretched out in perfect focus. He could see lines of roads, little insect dots that must have been cars. The blur beyond the desert was very definitely a mountain range on the horizon. The solitary shadow of the Divine Watch painted a gray triangle across the sands, and the shadow's tip rested on a tiny sliver of rock that stood up like a hairline spike in the distant mountain range.

"I can see it!" screamed Kevin, only half believing.

"What?" asked Josh.

"The Devil's Chair! Just like Kirkpatrick said! Just like he said!"

"How can you see anything?" asked Hal. "You're as blind as a bat!"

Josh's eyes cleared the top and he scanned the horizon.

"I don't see a thing!" said Josh. "It's too hazy!"

Kevin tried to climb higher, daring to actually stand atop the Divine Watch, but it was not meant to be. He was in too much of a hurry; he moved too quickly and lost his balance.

Kevin fell onto Josh, who toppled onto Hal, who crashed into Bertram, and the foursome plunged down the rocky cliff, rolling over sharp rocks and over each other until they smashed against a hard plateau fifty feet below.

At ten A.M., Bertram came into camp with a long scrape on his arm and skinned knees. He was followed by Hal, who was limping, and Josh, who had a cut on his face and scratched-up hands, and Kevin, who, having landed on Bertram, was completely unharmed.

For the entire trip back, Kevin had been all smiles. He had seen the top of the Watch, survived the climb, and acquired a souvenir to boot—and Bertram, who was too tired to beat him up at this point, would not get his hands on *these* glasses.

There was an uncanny, unpleasant sense that their experience on the mountain had somehow linked the four of them together like prisoners in a chain gang, but no one talked about it. No one talked much at all on the way back.

The boys marched into camp, looking like the sole survivors of a major plane crash, and they made their way to their tents. No one had noticed their disappearance, and no one noticed their return—what with so many kids running this way and that, throwing up Kirkpatrick's Chili-Eggs Scrambled with Garlic Over an Open Fire.

They wearily went to their tents to get a few minutes of sleep before they were dragged out for the day's festivities.

# CHAPTER 4

# Kevin Finds
# Rocks in His Head

Rumors spread, as rumors do, at the speed of light squared, and the buzz around the campsite focused on a single question:

*Could it possibly be true?*

Could they have climbed the Divine Watch, and could Kevin Midas actually have gotten there first?

Bertram denied that it ever happened. He would rather lie than allow Kevin the smallest glimpse of glory.

"But what about Josh's cut and Hal's bruises? What about my glasses?" Kevin tried to reason with the doubters.

"I can explain all that," said Nicole Patterson, who could always be counted on to explain all things. "Hal's a clumsy ox," she said. "If he *wasn't* bruised all the time I'd be surprised. Josh has a cut because Bertram must have slammed his face into a tree or something—and you must have found those glasses under a bush."

Kevin knew he'd never change her mind, so instead he just pushed his glasses farther up on his nose and asked proudly, "Do you like them?"

Nicole pondered them and shrugged. "They'd look a lot better on a larger head," she said.

And so until about three o'clock that afternoon, Kevin's life was pretty much unchanged.

At three, Bertram did some diving.

The assignment that afternoon was to do something that Native Americans might have done a thousand years ago. Most kids were spread out around a large, ice-cold pond near the campsite. Some hunted fish unsuccessfully with sharp sticks. Some ground berries into war paint, others were doing a sad-looking rain dance, and the rest watched with deep dread as Kirkpatrick cooked a snack of stir-fried forest-findings.

Kevin and Josh were lying on a boulder overlooking the pond.

"We're studying the clouds for a message from the sun-god," they told Kirkpatrick, "like Native Americans might have done." Kirkpatrick bought it and let them spend the afternoon basking in the sun, resting their aching feet.

Kevin basked with his glasses on. Through the dark lenses, he could see Josh staring at him. Josh was examining the glasses the way he would stare at a brand-new sports car, letting his eyes move across the perfect surface.

"You know," said Josh, "they could have been mine if I got there first."

Kevin shrugged. "That's the breaks."

"Your parents'll probably hate them," said Josh.

Kevin wondered if they'd even notice them. His mother rarely seemed to notice anything Kevin did, and his father was still trying to figure Kevin out.

"They won't care," said Kevin.

"You think Nicole likes your glasses?" he asked with a grin.

Kevin frowned. "She thinks I have a pinhead."

"You do," said Josh. "But that's okay, because you've also got a pin body."

Kevin was searching for a comeback line when Bertram called to them from across the pond.

"Hey," bellowed Bertram. "Hey, Midas, I hope you know I'm not talking to you because of what you did!"

Kevin, with the safety of a small lake between them, bellowed back, "Are you saying that you *admit* we climbed the mountain, and I got there first?"

"We admit nothing!" bellowed Hal, who stood firmly and strongly in Bertram's shadow.

"All's we admit," said Bertram, "is that you and Wilson are gonna have a short life expectancy unless you stay out of my way."

"Ah, go jump in a lake," said Kevin.

And sure enough, Bertram flung out his arms

and did a commanding belly flop into the frigid water.

When he surfaced and scrambled for shore, both Kevin and Josh broke out in raucous laughter. It was echoed by everyone else in attendance.

Bertram climbed out of the water and onto the boulder he had been standing on, trying to figure out what had happened.

"Hey, Bertràm," yelled Kevin, pushing the glasses farther up on his face, "that was pretty good—but can you do it again?"

Bertram slipped, spun his arms a few times, and flew into the lake once more. *Splash!* Everyone watching collapsed into convulsions.

Bertram blubbered his way to shore, only to find Hal laughing, too.

"Hey, Bertram," said Hal, "don't look now, but I think there's a fish in your pants."

Bertram then screamed his guts out, because, as everyone knew, Bertram was deathly afraid of live fish, due to some early-childhood trauma. He leapt around like a madman, until finally a small bull-head trout came flopping out the leg of his jeans.

Kevin and Josh were in stitches, but when they finally recovered enough to look at Bertram's face, they realized he had quickly overcome his terror. His fists were clenched, his jaw was clenched, and there was an evil look in his eyes—"the chain-saw look," as people called it. Bertram left his rock and began to run around the lake toward them, picking up speed like a locomotive. Hal ran around the lake the other way.

The sight of the rapidly approaching chain saw quickly sobered Kevin and Josh. They turned and raced barefoot into the woods.

"Nice going, Kevin," Josh hissed.

Kevin made it to safety, but Josh, whose feet were more swollen than Kevin's, was snatched by Hal and put into an Extremely Full Nelson.

Kevin hid behind an outcropping of boulders, waiting for an opportunity to spring Josh, and watched as a soaking-wet Bertram came into the clearing.

"You laughed at me?" Bertram screeched into Josh's face like a psychotic drill sergeant.

"No," said Josh, "we were laughing *with* you."

"You thought that was funny? The thing with the f-f-fish?"

Try as he might, Josh couldn't hold back his smile.

Bertram took Josh's arm and tugged it hard enough to send him sprawling in the dust.

"But what about Midas?" asked Hal.

"One at a time," said Bertram, flashing his teeth in a wide, crooked smile. "And I don't care what the teachers do to me, I don't care what my father does to me, and I don't even care if Midas calls out his big sister on me." Bertram pulled Josh to his feet and began to swing a heavy fist at Josh's nose.

Kevin had to think fast. There had to be a way to get out of this mess. Josh ducked, missing the first punch, but Bertram swung again.

Kevin didn't have time for a brainstorm, so a moderate brain drizzle would have to do. With all of his might he leaned against one of the boulders in front of him, until it crashed to the ground with a thud.

"Avalanche!" said Kevin.

"Huh?"

Bertram and Hal were distracted for only an instant, but that's all it took for Josh to slip away.

Kevin and Josh ran off together, thinking they had made an easy escape.

Then they saw a storm of boulders smashing down the slope toward them.

Suddenly Bertram didn't care about who had been laughing at him. He and Hal took off as the rumble around them grew louder and the boulders pounded closer.

Josh turned to run as fast as his legs could carry him, but Kevin just stood there, like a rabbit frozen on the highway, watching doom approach at sixty miles per hour.

Kevin's particular doom was a boulder twice his size, pounding down the mountain. He watched as it bounced toward him. It flattened a tree stump, then hit a sharp rock and split in two. The boulder parted around Kevin, brushing both his shoulders at the same time.

When Kevin turned, he saw Josh, who looked like a bowling pin with legs as he danced to avoid the stones rolling toward him. When the last of the boulders had passed, Josh breathed a sigh of relief and began screaming at Kevin.

"What's your problem?" yelled Josh. "Why did you just stand there?"

Kevin felt nothing—not fear, not anger. He felt numb—one hundred percent numb.

He spoke very slowly. "There was no avalanche, Josh."

Josh caught his breath and tried to stop shaking. "What do you call this? A hailstorm?"

"Well, yeah, there *was* an avalanche," said Kevin, "but I mean there wasn't an avalanche when I said there was."

"Yeah?" said Josh. "Well, maybe the rocks just fell out of your pinhead!"

The glasses had fallen during the avalanche, and when Kevin picked them up they were hot, as if they had been in the sun too long.

"It's lucky they weren't smashed," said Kevin.

"It's lucky *we* weren't smashed," said Josh, looking around him. "Let's get out of here. This spot must get avalanches all the time."

But Kevin knew that wasn't the case.

# CHAPTER 5

# Unmerciful
# Chocolate Destruction

The moment the avalanche ended, a storm began brewing in Kevin's mind.

While everyone jabbered on about the avalanche, and while the teachers thanked their Maker that no one was hurt by it, Kevin sat alone on one of the fallen boulders and stared with steely concentration at the mountain. It seemed robbed of its color today, remaining chalky white at sunset. The glasses, however, burned a silvery orange.

The thoughts swimming in Kevin's mind could have been products of his overactive imagination or the result of a lack of sleep and digestible food, but Kevin had a growing sense that something more was at work here. After the events of this afternoon, he was finding it harder and harder to believe that his glasses had been left behind on the mountain by some ultracool hiker who wanted to stake a claim.

"What would you say, Josh, if I told you that

these glasses were magic?" Kevin whispered as he and Josh waited in the long dinner line.

"I would say you've been reading too many comic books."

The line crept slowly toward Mr. Kirkpatrick, who was dishing up some slop everyone was calling Hamburger Helpless.

"What if I told you I could prove it?" asked Kevin.

"Then I would say the avalanche knocked some of your screws loose."

Kevin knew that Josh was the kind of kid who wouldn't believe anything until he saw it. So Kevin grabbed his arm and pulled him out of line.

"Hey, what's the idea?" yelled Josh. "I haven't eaten all day. I'm starved!"

"Follow me. It'll only take a second." Kevin led Josh off into the woods until the sounds from the campsite were far away, and he was sure no one could hear them.

"Okay," said Kevin. "Here's the proof: One, I told Bertram to jump in the lake, and he did."

"Big deal."

"Two, I told him to do it again, and he did it again!"

"Big deal."

"Three, the avalanche. I said there was an avalanche, and then, *pow*, there was one."

Josh leaned against a tree, and a look of worry

began to creep onto his face. "What you're saying is looney-toons, you know that?"

Kevin took off the glasses and looked at them. Now they had faded to the rich purple of the western sky.

"They tingle, Josh."

"What?"

"The glasses. They tingle. First, when I told Bertram to jump, and then when I said, 'Avalanche.' They tingled ... and it sort of felt ... good."

Josh reached out his hand. "Let me see."

"No!" Kevin pushed Josh's hand away. Josh frowned but didn't reach for them again.

"What do you want me to do, then?" asked Josh.

Kevin's voice was a whisper. "Ask me to wish for something."

"You're nuts."

"Ask me."

"You're certifiable!"

"What are you afraid of?"

It was a good question, and rather than admit he was afraid, Josh gave Kevin a wish.

"An ice-cream cone," said Josh.

"What flavor?"

"Unmerciful Chocolate Destruction. A double scoop."

"Cake cone or sugar cone?"

"Just get it over with!"

Kevin planted his feet firmly on the ground and

stuck out his hand, concentrating with the full force of his mind.

"Okay," said Kevin, "give me one double dip of Unmerciful Chocolate Destruction on a sugar cone to go!"

The glasses went dark, and at first Kevin could see nothing. Then a spot of light appeared before him, which exploded in waves of brilliant color. He could feel the warmth and tingle of the frames as they ever so slightly surged with energy, as if they were pulling it right out of Kevin's head.

"Kevin," said Josh, his voice trembling, "your eyes . . . I think they're glowing!"

In his mind, Kevin imagined the cone dripping with ice cream, and then, when the colors faded from before his eyes, he realized that the picture he had in his mind had entered the real world.

Unmerciful Chocolate Destruction dripped down his fingers, cold and sticky.

Josh was the first to scream, and Kevin joined him. He dropped the cone and they both ran from it, screaming at the top of their lungs, until they got to a clearing far away from the horrific cone. There they stopped to catch their breath.

"This is weird, Kevin!"

"I know!"

"No, I mean this is *really* weird. Remember when Ralphy Sherman said his father was a werewolf, and then they found him one morning sleeping in a neighbor's doghouse? Well, *this* is weirder."

Kevin looked at his hand, which still had some melted chocolate ice cream on it. He licked it. It was unmercifully real.

"What are we gonna do?" asked Josh. "What are we gonna do?" And then something struck him. "Hey," asked Josh, "where's my ice-cream cone?"

With Hamburger Helpless on the menu, it quickly became obvious what they were going to do. If reality was flexible enough to allow an ice-cream cone to be born out of thin air, then it was flexible enough for quite a variety of things.

Within ten minutes the little clearing was filled with food. Burgers from every imaginable fast-food chain lay all over the ground, one bite taken from each. The birds were feasting on french fries, and a bivouac of army ants was all but carrying away the discarded burgers.

And, of course, the feast was topped off by a whole gallon barrel of U.C.D. ice cream. They kept shoveling in the ice cream until it could no longer go down and just sort of squirted out of the sides of their mouths when they tried to swallow. Then they rested; two beached whales barely able to move.

The glasses, which had gotten a bit warm when Kevin wished up their gluttonous feast, had cooled off. Now, in the moonlit sky, their tint seemed to have disappeared, leaving the lenses completely clear.

"This is just the beginning." Kevin took off his glasses and polished them against his shirt. "There's no limit to the things we can wish up!"

"Yeah," said Josh. "But what if it's not all free?"

"Like how?"

"What if the glasses are like some ... I don't know ... like some intergalactic charge card, or something? And what if someone comes to collect the bill?"

"They don't work like that," said Kevin.

"How do you know?"

"Because I do! When you wear the glasses, you just know things about them."

"Like what?"

Kevin cradled the glasses in his hands, running his fingers tenderly across the black-and-gold rim.

"Like they were meant to be used," he said. "Like they're supposed to make everything a whole lot better. That they're more valuable than anything in the world."

Josh reached out and gently took the glasses from Kevin, staring at them as if he held the world's most precious diamond in his hands. He seemed almost afraid to be touching them.

"Would I feel all that if *I* wore them?" asked Josh.

"Probably," said Kevin, grabbing the glasses back and slipping them on. "But you don't need to wear them, as long as you've got me. I'll give you whatever you want."

Josh seemed relieved, as if he really didn't want to test them himself, anyway.

Kevin burped, then giggled as a thought occurred to him. "I guess I'm the master of the universe."

"Ah, put a leash on it!" said Josh.

"No way." Kevin's imagination had been strapped to a post long enough. He stood up, hungry for something more than fast food, and climbed on a high boulder, reaching a hand up to the heavens.

Josh laughed. "Whatcha gonna do? Part the Red Sea?"

"Something like that."

Josh stopped laughing and watched as Kevin stared through his glasses at the infinite depths of the star-filled sky.

"Clouds," he whispered to the night. The frame of the glasses began to get warm, the lenses went dark and then silver. Directly above them, a gray spot appeared, like a hole in the sky, and clouds began to unfold, growing high above their heads—dense gray clouds, but the glasses reflected them in rich, swirling hues.

"Pretty intense," said Josh. "Now stop it."

The clouds spread out and blackened. Now the entire mountain was covered by gray clouds, turning black. A billow shrouded the moon, and the forest became as dark as moonshadow. Kevin held both hands up to the sky. "Wind!" he said. And the mountain breathed, sending a wind that rasped across the treetops, then swooped down, picking up leaves and pine needles, dragging them away.

Josh labored against his full stomach to stand up. "Are you deaf? I said that's enough!"

"Faster!" Kevin said. The wind began to groan and the trees bend to its voice.

Back at the campsite, everyone must have been watching the dark threat of the sky. Kevin could imagine tents blowing away with the wind, *his* wind.

"You see?" said Kevin. "All I have to do is say it, and it happens! Even if I just whisper it!" Far above, the clouds began to flash and rumble.

"Kevin, you're scaring me!" yelled Josh. "Stop it!"

"I'm not finished!" It was Christmas rolled up with the Fourth of July. The clouds began to swirl and change, their electricity moaning to be released.

Now the smile was gone from Kevin's face, and although the glasses had gone as dark as dark could be, Kevin could see through them with an impossible clarity. He could see all the clouds, inside and out, swirling with color. The eyeglass frame was heating up around his ears and across his eyebrows. It glowed a dull red. "Now the fireworks!" He threw up his hands like the very small conductor of a very large orchestra.

"Lightning," he said.

"Kevin, no!"

Lightning exploded all around them.

Again Kevin threw up his hands and pulled down the lightning, much more violently than before. Now it was time for the grand finale. He pointed his finger at a tree directly in front of him. "There!" he said, and as he did, a fat, sizzling bolt shot down from the sky, hit the tree dead center, and split it in two with a deafening roar.

The colors swirling before his eyes settled down as the glasses awaited their next command—but Kevin had had enough for now. He let the colors fade and the glasses wash clear once more. He took off the glasses and admired his masterpiece raging in the clouds all around them. "So, how did you like that?" Kevin asked. He turned to see Josh crumpled in a ball, shaking, with his hands over his head as if it were the end of the world.

"Make it go away!" he wailed as the storm continued to build. "*Please* make it stop."

"Ah, don't be so gutless." Kevin pushed the glasses farther up on his nose and reached up his hands. "No more lightning," he said.

A moment later, lightning struck again.

"I said make it stop!" yelled Josh.

"I'm trying!" Kevin threw up his hands and

called out in his most powerful voice, "No more storm!"

But neither the glasses nor the sky seemed to listen. The wind blew, the lightning crashed, and the clouds kept bubbling slowly outward.

"What's wrong?"

"I don't know! I don't know, it's not working anymore!" Small drops of rain began to fall on them, and then the clouds ruptured like a water balloon, letting loose a downpour the likes of which the mountain had never seen.

"Let's get out of here!" Josh yelled over the roar of thunder. They ran from the clearing just a moment before it was blasted by lightning.

The camping trip was ruined. When the lightning started, everyone raced for the vans. Kevin and Josh were the last to arrive. For a half hour, everyone huddled in the vans, filled with a weird sort of excitement, as they wondered whether or not they were all going to die in a flash flood. The kids who had done the rain dance earlier that day proudly claimed responsibility.

After an hour, it became clear that waiting out the storm was more dangerous than driving through it, and so the teachers ventured out to collect what was left of the tents. The rain was still coming down in sheets when the vans crawled out of the campsite.

Kevin leaned his head against the cold window

and wiped the fog off the glass. As they put more distance between them and the Divine Watch, the thunder began to chase the lightning, falling farther and farther behind with each flash. Kevin had to smile. To think that this was all his doing!

"There's nothing funny about it," said Josh. And that's all he had to say. On Josh's video game, fighter jets bombed Godzilla. By his score, Kevin could tell Josh really wasn't concentrating.

Only fifteen minutes after the bus had left the Divine Watch, they finally passed out of the storm, and the normal, comfortable chaos filled the van. Kevin was not a part of it. He felt far away. As numb as the chilling rain. As smooth as the surface of his glasses.

"I know why I couldn't stop the storm," Kevin told Josh, when they were well away from the Divine Watch.

"Why?"

"I don't think the glasses can reverse what I've asked them to do; they can't *uncreate* anything they've created."

"So is it going to rain there forever?"

Kevin shrugged. "I guess."

"You guess?" said Josh. "You turn a mountain into a rain forest, and all you can say is 'I guess'?"

Kevin didn't know what else to say to Josh, so instead he pushed the glasses up snugly on his face and reached out his hand. "Hey, Josh?"

Josh turned to Kevin, and Kevin touched the

piece of gauze on Josh's cheek that covered the cut he got when they fell from the mountain.

"Heal," whispered Kevin. He imagined the cut on Josh's face gone and then slowly peeled off the bandage. There was no sign Josh had ever been cut at all.

"See, Josh? The glasses can do good things, too. It just depends on how you want to use them." Josh still didn't say anything. "So, are we still friends?" asked Kevin.

Josh looked at Kevin and thought for a moment. He reached out, took the glasses off Kevin's face, and put them in Kevin's jacket pocket, zipping the pocket completely closed.

"Of course we're still friends," he said.

Kevin felt the glasses bulging in his jacket, and for a moment he wanted to feel their weight on the bridge of his nose again—but his head was beginning to ache just a bit, and he figured they should stay in his pocket for a while.

Behind them the storm faded on the horizon until it was out of sight and out of mind. Two girls in the front were glancing at Kevin and laughing about the way his face had gotten sunburned everywhere except around his eyes—but it was all right. It didn't matter what anyone said or did to him now. Because now, Kevin was finally in control.

# CHAPTER 6

# *Better Homes and Headaches*

It was the usual Monday morning madhouse.

Downstairs the TV blared, and the dog was barking nonstop. In the master bedroom, the electric razor buzzed as Patrick Midas, Kevin's father, made his magical transition from stubble-bearded bum into clean-shaven businessman. In the hall bathroom, Teri Midas, Kevin's fourteen-year-old sister, blasted a radio while blasting her wet head with hot air. And, as if all this noise wasn't enough, Monday was trash day.

Kevin cringed in bed as a metal garbage can rang out like a broken bell. No doubt trash collectors' pay was based on how much noise they could make.

"Avalanches!" said Donna Midas, Kevin's mom. "Avalanches and rainstorms!" She violently shook a thermometer and crammed it into Kevin's mouth. "Avalanches, rainstorms, and camping trips! You're going to kill me one of these days, Kevin, you know that?"

Kevin knew he didn't have a fever, but he did have a splitting headache and no intention of going to school today.

"I warned you not to overexert yourself," she said. "But does Kevin Brian Midas listen to anyone but himself? No!—and don't you dare talk! The last thing I need is for you to bite that thermometer and die of mercury poisoning."

She glanced at her watch. "Late again," she muttered as she hurried out of the room.

The second she was gone, Kevin ran over to his desk, grabbed his glasses out of the top drawer, and put them on.

"Great shades," said Teri as she passed by with a toothbrush in her mouth. "Where'd you steal 'em?"

"I didn't steal them, I found them," said Kevin, around his thermometer.

Teri frothed at the mouth. "I'll tell you what. If you let me borrow them for a couple of days, I'll convince Mom that you're sick enough to stay home."

"No deal."

Teri shrugged and sauntered off. "Suit yourself."

Kevin heard her spit in the bathroom sink. Teri, by being the smallest yet toughest field-hockey goalie Ridgeline Middle School had ever seen, had developed a callous self-confidence, and she often used it to make Kevin feel uncomfortable. She would glance at him with a smirk, and the mere glance would make Kevin wonder if he had two different socks on or if his fly were open. She would say things like "Suit yourself" and saunter off as if she knew something Kevin didn't, causing Kevin to give in. Right now, she was probably counting the seconds until Kevin returned to the bargaining table. But this time, no deal meant no deal.

With the glasses on, Kevin's headache was already subsiding, so he dressed quickly and went downstairs to make himself some breakfast.

The TV in the living room blared the news, and the family dog, as was its peculiar custom, barked at the people on the screen as if they were strangers invading its home. Kevin took a detour through the living room because the news report was about the storm around the Divine Watch. Although the dog made it difficult to hear, Kevin did pick up some of it.

"*The storm* (BARK, BARK) *several power outages* (BARK, BARK) *flash floods throughout the entire* (BARK) *and is slowly spreading outward.* (BARK, GROWL, BARK)"

"Will somebody muzzle the Muffler?" yelled Teri from upstairs.

"Shut up, Muffy," Kevin said to the beagle. The glasses flashed, and Muffy continued barking, but no sound came out.

"There you are," said Mrs. Midas, plucking the thermometer out of Kevin's mouth. "Ninety-eight point six," she reported. "Perfectly normal."

"Send him to school, he's not sick," said Teri, throwing Kevin a sideways glance as she came downstairs.

Kevin pushed the glasses up on the bridge of his nose. "It says one hundred and one."

Mrs. Midas glanced at the thermometer again. "That's strange—it *does* say a hundred and one. I must have misread it.

Kevin gave Teri a smirk. `

"Score one for you," said Teri, genuinely surprised. "I hope you feel better, Kev."

As Mrs. Midas shoved the thermometer back in Kevin's mouth to see if it would climb any higher, Mr. Midas flew down the stairs. He headed straight for the fridge, where he grabbed a box of chocolate doughnuts—his usual breakfast. Having already gone on his morning run, he had bought himself the right to all the poor eating habits the day offered.

"Your son's got a fever," said Kevin's mom, who always referred to Kevin as "your son" when it was something bad and "my son" when it was something good.

"I'll alert the media," said Mr. Midas, his mouth full of doughnut. He felt Kevin's head, pulled the thermometer from his mouth, examined it, and asked his wife why on earth she was using the rectal thermometer.

As usual, Josh had waited patiently for Kevin to show up at his door, but he finally gave up and came by to see what was keeping him. Even before he arrived, Josh had a sneaking suspicion that school was not on Kevin's list of the day's activities.

Kevin was wearing the glasses when he opened the door, and Josh could tell by the relative quiet that everyone else had gone.

"I guess you didn't tell anyone about the glasses," said Josh.

"Are you kidding me?" answered Kevin. "Why ruin a perfect day?"

As he passed the living room, Josh noticed Muffy silently opening and closing her yap at the TV screen. "What's wrong with the Muffler?" asked Josh.

"I told her to shut up," said Kevin.

"Good dog!" commented Josh. "C'mon, hurry up, we're already late."

"No school," said Kevin. "I'm staying home to conduct a science experiment today." He hurried off into the kitchen.

The kitchen table was covered with the Sunday paper, dissected and examined for every single advertisement that seemed the slightest bit interesting, from grand openings of electronics stores to beef sales at the supermarket. Kevin had already begun circling the more promising ones with a red pen.

"What sort of experiment?" As if Josh really needed to ask.

"Sit down," said Kevin, "and start picking things you want." Josh didn't sit down just yet, but he did begin to examine the ads cautiously. There was a picture of a stereo system that must have stood a foot taller than he was. It was the sort of system Josh dreamed about.

"You know," said Josh, "it's still raining. . . ."

"I don't see any rain."

"You know what I mean!"

Kevin shrugged it off. "So? It's only a storm. How long can it last?"

Josh examined the sleek digital stereo system that advertised sound reproduction of such superior quality that it actually reproduced sounds out of the range of human hearing. Its price was out of the range of human comprehension.

"I've got to get to school," said Josh, although he didn't put down the ad.

"C'mon." Kevin took a damp paper towel and gently cleaned his precious lenses. "Let's treat ourselves to something."

"Okay," said Josh. "One thing."

"Right."

"One for you, and one for me."

"Okay," said Kevin. "Two things."

"Right," said Josh. "What are you getting?"

Kevin pointed to the ad in Josh's hand. "That stereo right there."

"Great. I want that, too."

"But that's just two of the same thing," said

Kevin. "It's just like *one* thing, and we agreed we'd get *two* things."

"Okay, one more thing then."

"Fine," said Kevin.

"One for you and one for me," added Josh.

"And that's all."

"Right. Just these four things, and that's all."

"Okay."

"Okay."

Within five minutes the experiment was raging out of control, and neither of them got to school that day. The only limits to what could be dreamt up were the clarity of Kevin's thoughts and the speed at which he could speak them into existence.

First came the stereo systems—a half dozen of them, because, with further browsing, they weren't quite sure which they wanted—the ones with multi-megawatt speakers so small they could fit in the palm of your hand or the ones so large they took up an entire wall. They kept ordering up televisions as they found bigger and better ones on each page.

Eventually they ran out of electronics and went on to furniture, then to clothing. When they ran out of advertisements, they began scouring household magazines for pictures that would spark their imaginations.

"Hey, Kevin, look at this!" Josh had dug up one of Mr. Midas's *Playboy*s, which had always been kept hidden from Kevin. The very idea turned Kevin beet red, and he began to giggle. "No," said Kevin, "maybe not."

"Maybe later?"

"Yeah, maybe later."

The magazine remained in the living room all day, but neither of them dared to go near it.

By noon, Josh noticed that the temperature in the house had begun to drop, but he didn't say anything—he didn't think it meant much. Kevin, on the other hand, wouldn't have noticed if the sky were falling—his attention was elsewhere. Beneath it all, Kevin knew he had a headache again, but as long as the glasses stayed hot and he kept them active, every inch of his body and mind felt so tingly and electrified that he didn't care about how his head would feel when he stopped.

They rode their bikes down to the mall and went on a window-shopping spree, duplicating half the things they saw and wishing them back to Kevin's house, including their favorite games in the video arcade.

When they arrived back home, they had to climb in a side window because one of their home-theater systems was blocking the front door.

At last they took a break from the experiment. Kevin, drained and exhausted, took off the glasses and flopped onto his bed, but Josh, having been baptized into fantasyland, and still submerged in its rich, sweet waters, danced to the music that rocked the entire house as he made his way around the obstacle course in Kevin's room.

"Santa Claus better watch his butt!" said Josh. "The dude's got competition now!" Josh swung open the door to Kevin's closet, revealing a soft-drink machine, which, of course, didn't require money to operate. Josh got himself a Dr Pepper, leapt onto Kevin's desk, and twanged an awful chord on a star-spangled guitar, spilling soda foam all over.

"And it's all tax free!" said Josh. He jumped in the air, twanged the guitar, and came crashing down on a pinball machine that began to blink "tilt."

"I need some aspirin," said Kevin. "I need some Pepto-Bismol."

"If you feel sick, why don't you just wish it away?"

"I tried," said Kevin. "The glasses made me sick—they can't un-make me sick."

Josh slowed down and began to catch his breath from his whirlwind romance with greed. The house felt chilly. No—not just chilly, it felt cold, and Kevin—well, Kevin looked cold. He had wrapped himself in a blanket and was shivering slightly.

Kevin was ready to call it a day, and Josh would have agreed—until Josh turned his eyes just a few feet up and saw the poster hanging so innocently above Kevin's bed.

"One more thing," said Josh.

"I'm fried," said Kevin.

Josh smiled. "Too fried for the car of your dreams?"

Kevin sat up slowly. He thought about it, then hesitated. "Give me the glasses, and I'll do it," said Josh.

"No!" Kevin grabbed the glasses from his nightstand and put them on.

It was called the Lamborghini Countach, and it was the subject of most of Kevin's classroom doodles. Kevin, fighting exhaustion, raced down the stairs with Josh and into the garage.

"I never even thought I'd ever *see* a Lamber-geenie, and now I'm going to have one," said Kevin.

Josh shook his head. "How many times do I have to tell you? It's not Lam-ber-geenie, it's *Lamborghini!* You have to think Italian!"

The garage was empty except for the ancient junk against the wall and two oil spots where his parents' cars had been. Kevin had turned the stereo off on the way through the living room, so the only sound came from the heater in the corner of the garage. It hummed, showing traces of flames as it tried unsuccessfully to warm the unseasonably cold house.

"We'll get two of them," said Josh. "Okay?"

"One for you and one for me, right?"

"Right."

"Okay."

Kevin took a deep breath, cleared his throat, and said the words, which echoed in the empty garage.

"Two red Lam-ber-geenies."

*"Lamborghinis!"*

"Yeah, yeah."

The colors before Kevin's eyes began to swirl, and he felt as though his whole brain was filtering out through the dark glass.

From where Josh stood, the sight of the glasses at work was just as remarkable, and although he had seen it before, each time was better than the last. Josh watched as the glasses got so dark that they looked like portals into another universe. Deep within that universe, Josh saw Kevin's eye burning like blue flames. From this side of the glasses, Kevin's mind seemed like something impossibly huge, and almost as a reflex, Josh grabbed tightly onto a bicycle hook in the wall for fear of being sucked right in through the glasses. Blinding colors pulsed out from the glasses, and Josh had to shield his eyes.

When he looked again, there were two Lamborghinis just sitting in the garage as if they had no better place to be.

Josh let go of the hook, leapt into the window of the nearest one, and sank into the seat. Keys were in the ignition, and he wished with all his heart that he knew how to drive.

Kevin wasn't as quick to get into his car. As his

trembling hand removed the red-hot glasses, he could feel his heart pulsing in the tiny veins in his eyeballs and knew his eyes must have been bloodshot beyond belief. His head swam and ached as if someone had reached inside and pulled the two cars right out of his skull. He felt very, very cold.

Kevin got into his car and sat down, feeling the smooth leather against his aching body. He looked toward Josh, and they both noticed something at the same time. It was so cold in the garage that their breath came out in puffs of steam.

Kevin looked around, to find everything in the garage frozen. An icicle dripped from the leaky spigot, and the puddle beneath it was a sheet of ice. Even the heater had been snuffed out. It must have been twenty degrees in that garage!

*It's a side effect*, thought Kevin. The glasses needed lots of energy to work, and they stole energy wherever they could find it. Heat, light, fire. The glasses just sucked the heat right out of the air!

Kevin and Josh sat in the freezing garage, playing behind the wheels of their twin Lamborghinis for a while, until Josh finally turned to Kevin.

"So now what?"

Amazingly enough, Kevin couldn't answer him. Now they had everything. They had wished up *everything* their hearts desired, from the smallest toy to the largest. The house was piled to the ceiling with *things*.

Having played the video games, listened to the stereos, watched the home theaters, tried the candy machines, tasted all the food, worn all the clothes, sat on all the couches, and played in both the cars—after all that—they were finally bored. So now what? . . . So *now* what?

Kevin racked his aching brain for something else that he wanted but couldn't find it. The world of goods and services had nothing more to offer.

And then a thought occurred to Kevin that put everything into a slightly different perspective.

"What am I going to tell my parents?"

Josh looked up from his dashboard. "Yeah," he said, "what *are* you going to tell your parents about all this stuff?"

Kevin looked down at his new gold Rolex watch. It was five-fifteen, and his mom, who was never on time going to work but always on time getting back, picked up Teri from field hockey practice promptly at five. They were due home any second.

Back in the house, Muffy cowered behind a jukebox. The place was a disaster area, as if someone had crammed a mansion into a three-bedroom home. The obvious excuses passed quickly through Kevin's mind as he felt panic take hold.

*It was like this when I got here.* Did he really think they would buy that, knowing full well that he stayed home from school today?

*We won it on a game show.* What game show? How? Where? What a lame story.

*Remember when the sweepstakes letter said "You May Already Be a Winner"?* No, no, no! What was he going to do? Practically paralyzed by panic, Kevin sat at the foot of the stairs and watched as Josh paced a short path in the over-stuffed room.

"We can't let them know! You've got to make it go away!" said Josh. "Wish it all back!"

"I can't," croaked Kevin. "You know the glasses can't undo what they've done." Kevin heard the troubled engine of his mother's Volvo backfire down the street. It was the only warning they got—and Kevin figured they had ten seconds, tops.

"Quick," said Josh, "do something! *Your* parents will just have heart attacks when they see this stuff, but mine will have heart attacks *and* give me a double-lifetime grounding without possibility of parole, no matter what the explanation is! DO SOMETHING."

"What?"

"If you can't just lose the stuff, then send it somewhere else!"

"Where?"

"ANYWHERE!"

The electric garage door opener cranked into action. Kevin could hear the car pulling up the driveway.

Kevin stood up, and without a second to lose,

held his head together to keep it from splitting and made a desperate wish.

"Uhh. . . . Uh . . .."

"Hurry!"

"Uh . . . everything that I made today, go . . . *Go next door!*"

First came the blackness, then the colors, then the fingers reaching into his brain, and a flash of light. Kevin screamed, threw the glasses from his face, and they fell down upon . . .

. . . an empty floor.

The house was exactly the way it was before they had begun their shopping spree. The same old TV. The same old furniture. Everything else was gone.

Mrs. Midas's car backfired once as it pulled into the empty garage.

There was a rumble then—a shaking of the ground and a creaking of wood, like an earthquake. Kevin and Josh raced out the front door in time to see it happen.

The house next door was a small home owned by the Kimballs, a pleasant elderly couple who never bothered anyone. The Kimball place was half the size of the Midas home and would not have the space for all the things Kevin had so hurriedly wished upon it.

Mrs. Kimball, sitting quietly on the front porch, could only watch as the walls began to buckle outward. Upstairs a frozen-yogurt machine expanded through a window and crashed to the ground with the shattering of glass.

A grand piano bounced through the side of the house, landing in a flower bed, and the front door regurgitated stereo equipment, with a rasping of metal and plastic.

The front lawn began to ripple like an ocean as video games sprouted up from the earth, and from the garage came an awful crunching sound that could only be the two Lamborghinis flattening the old couple's Buick against the wall.

It ended with a blast of the chimney as hundreds of rare coins shot into the air, showering the neighborhood in shimmering gold and silver.

People came racing from their homes—but because it all happened so quickly, they could only see the results, not the cause.

"Cool!" said Teri, who had come out of the garage in time to witness the end of the spectacle. Kevin's mom could only stand and stare like the rest of the neighbors, who scratched their heads and looked to the skies as if some cargo jet had unexpectedly dumped its load.

Mrs. Kimball gazed around her with her hands on her hips, then slowly made her way down from the porch and calmly climbed around the various artifacts that littered her lawn.

She smiled at Kevin's mom and politely asked, "Excuse me, may I use your phone?"

Kevin's mom nodded, and the old woman quietly disappeared into their house.

Kevin watched from his bedroom window that night as lookey-loos from all over town gathered to watch a troop of movers organize everything on the Kimball's front lawn.

An insurance adjuster, one step short of falling into a coma, just stood there on the lawn and gaped for an hour.

There was applause when Mr. Kimball drove a Lamborghini out of the garage, and then Frankie Philpot showed up, as everyone knew he would. Frankie, a dentist with a burning interest in the supernatural, had his own local—if somewhat cheap—cable TV show, devoted entirely to psychic phenomena. Frankie and his dental hygienist video crew interviewed the Kimballs right beneath Kevin's window.

Frankie Philpot deduced that the Kimball house existed over a space-time wormhole thingy that somehow opened up into the Bermuda Triangle or a distant department store.

The insurance adjuster, for lack of any better explanation, decided that the Kimballs were victims of a hit-and-run delivery truck.

Everyone else just figured it was "one of those things" and eventually went home.

# CHAPTER 7

# Kevin Becoming

While certain other parts of the world may have been engulfed in storm clouds, the suburban town of Ridgeline awoke to a bright, sunny day.

The sun rose behind the electrical tower on the hill in back of Kevin Midas's home, casting shadows of the girders on Kevin's white walls. The room had stayed cold all night, defying the thermostat's attempts to keep it the same temperature as the rest of the house. Only now, as the morning light began to shine through the eastern window, did warmth return to Kevin's life.

All night he had stayed bundled under the many blankets that his mother always insisted he keep folded up on the end of his bed. When he awoke at dawn, he couldn't move a muscle without feeling incredible pangs shoot through his head and then ricochet down through the rest of his body.

He had gone straight to bed the night before, without eating, so he felt weak, and he could do little more than lie there and watch the slow progress of the girder shadows as they moved across the wall.

There was a buzzing around him—a hum that could barely be heard. At first he took it for his father's electric razor, and then for the buzz of the high-tension wires outside—until he realized that the sound was coming from his desk.

The glasses were there, resting six inches from the wall—six inches from an electrical outlet. Kevin watched in amazement as a line of blue electricity arced across the air from the outlet to the glasses.

*They're recharging,* Kevin realized. They had taken the heat from his room, but it wasn't enough. Now they were sucking the very electricity from the walls! *How much energy did they need?* Kevin wondered. *How much could they absorb?* Kevin reached out and took a pencil from his desk. With it he gently moved the glasses away from the wall until the electrical arc was broken. The glasses just sat there now, glistening in the morning sun.

Kevin then crawled out from underneath his covers like a slug from underneath a rock. While everyone else in the house still slept, he suffered through a shower that didn't make him feel the least bit better.

When he returned to his room, the glasses were waiting.

He put them on even before he dressed and instantly felt the change. It began with his eyes—a soothing feeling that slowly spread down and out, reaching the tips of his fingers and the soles of his feet. He closed his eyes and let the feeling wash through him. He was better now, and he couldn't imagine why he had waited this long to put the glasses back on.

He dressed in plain old jeans and a shirt, then stared at himself in the tall mirror against his closet door. Plain, ordinary, boring—that's how he looked. That's how he *always* looked. *There's no reason to dress like this,* Kevin thought. No reason at all. He could look like . . . he could *be* whoever or whatever he wanted.

The secret, Kevin figured, was not to ask for everything you ever wanted all at once, but just to ask for the right things at the right times.

He imagined what he wanted himself to be wearing—he could almost see it in the mirror—and then he said the words that dressed him head to toe. Kevin stared at himself in the mirror from all angles, admiring his flashy designer outfit, complete with brand-new basketball shoes, until he caught sight of Teri standing in the doorway behind him.

"What's with you?" she asked, morning gravel still in her throat.

"Nothing," said Kevin, casually flipping up the collar on his new leather jacket. "I'm checking out some new clothes—is there anything wrong with that?"

"You're such a basket case," she replied, both of them knowing full well that the true basket case was Teri, as she shuffled off with drooping eyelids toward the bathroom.

That morning Kevin joined his father on his morning jog—something Kevin had tried only once before. On that one occasion, Patrick Midas had driven Kevin to absolute exhaustion and then acted surprised when Kevin couldn't keep up.

His father, who liked to speak in short, meaningless phrases, always told Kevin, "No pain, no gain," and used that motto as an excuse to turn any father-and-son physical activity into a trial by fire for Kevin. Kevin was amazed that after all that, he still enjoyed sports as much as he did—although his best sport was soccer, the only sport his father absolutely detested.

With the glasses firmly affixed to his face and a well-placed wish on his lips, Kevin joined his father on the morning run and left the poor man in his dust. When Patrick Midas finally made it back to the front door, dripping with sweat and barely able to breathe, Kevin, already there, jogged in place, barely winded at all, and said, "No pain, no gain," with a shrug.

Before going inside, Kevin sat on the porch and watched the Kimballs for a while. Their house would never be the same, but perhaps that didn't matter, because the old couple was excitedly preparing for what would be the mother of all garage sales.

Things were different for Kevin in school. It began that very day and gradually took hold throughout the week. Perhaps it was the way he was dressed—or perhaps it was the way no one could see his eyes behind those intensely cool glasses that seemed to change color at will. Or maybe it was just self-confidence; a presence about him that made kids get out of his way when he walked down the hall, even though he was a head shorter than most.

Or maybe it was the way that he always seemed to have just what people needed when they needed it.

Kevin had never before had the guts to join in a conversation with kids who weren't his best buddies—but now that had changed.

Justin Gere, an eighth grader, was complaining to a couple of his friends that he had every major-league baseball card issued that year except Carlysle Sparks, one of the Dodgers' rarely used relief pitchers. Rumor was the card had never been printed.

"Well, wouldn't you know it!" said Kevin Midas. "I've got an extra one." He presented Carlysle Sparks to Justin as if he had pulled it out of his sleeve, which he had.

Alyssa Peevar was in tears because she had lost her charm bracelet down a deep storm drain that appeared to go all the way to China. The bracelet was, of course, lost forever, but Kevin reached down into the drain and produced it—or at least a good replica.

When Dash Kaminsky, who the girls claimed was drop-dead gorgeous, got his million-dollar lips smashed by a hockey puck, who was there with a handful of ice and a kind word that seemed to make the swelling go away in seconds? Kevin, of course.

In just a few days Kevin's popularity had grown like a vine on the brickwork of Ridgeline Middle School—quickly and silently, so that very few people remembered it being any different. Kevin had made the transition to everybody's buddy, and although he wasn't the most popular kid in school, people who would never have given him the time of day before suddenly said hello and didn't mind having him around.

It was clear to Kevin that things were changing—he was changing. But changing wasn't the right word. He was *becoming*. Becoming what? he wondered. He decided it didn't really matter, because whatever it was, it was better than what he had been before.

A few other people noticed Kevin's frightening transformation.

Josh was one. When Josh saw Kevin waltz in

that Tuesday morning after their ill-fated shopping spree, he knew right away that Kevin wasn't going to give the glasses a rest. Josh, who had admittedly been a little greed-meister the day before, had learned his lesson when it was crammed down his throat. The glasses were bad news. Period. But Kevin didn't get it.

"The storm's still growing," Josh would often remind Kevin.

"So, isn't there a drought?" Kevin would answer, letting the storm roll off the top of his head like water off Scotchguard. The truth was that the storm made the news every day. "An inland hurricane" was what they were now calling it. They named it Hurricane Gladys, but it should have been called Kevin.

Bertram also noticed Kevin's new station in life. Bertram would chew his pink cud and watch in disgust as Kevin actually chummed around with older, respectable kids.

In Bertram's book you were born into your place in life. Bertram's place was well guarded and well worn. He knew who he was and what was expected of him; he was and would always be the Mean Kid—and he liked that just fine.

But it seemed Kevin had forgotten who he was.

Kevin was the Victim. He had been the Victim since first grade, and someday in the far-off future, when Bertram was teaching his own kids all about being mean, Kevin Midas would be suffering some dumb life in some stupid boring town, the Victim of some big stupid company that would fire him for no good reason.

Thoughts like this kept Bertram going.

But seeing Kevin Midas succeeding—this didn't fit the Bertram World View. It made him chomping mad.

Kevin was wise to keep away from Bertram—and he did for three whole days. On Friday, however, the fine threads of Kevin's hand-made universe began to unravel.

# CHAPTER 8

## Kevin's Tangled Web

Winds blew in from the north that Friday—strange winds that swirled together, forming tiny candy-wrapper tornadoes on the baseball field.

It was all some distant effect of the inland hurricane, which still had meteorologists scratching their heads. These were the kinds of winds that stirred kids up, and like the others, Kevin had felt the itch of excitement, like static electricity, all morning.

During lunch, Kevin sat by himself beneath the flapping sails of a lunch-table umbrella. The rest of the week he had managed to surround himself with other kids, but since he was not producing an endless supply of goodies from his backpack today, no one was very interested in him.

That was fine with Kevin, because he had a plan to weave. He stared out into the baseball field, where kids were sitting in small groups eating their lunches, and he thought long and hard.

"I'd like it a lot better if I could see your eyes," said Josh as he took a seat next to Kevin. "What's so interesting out in right field?"

Kevin took off his glasses and squinted at Josh. "Nicole Patterson."

"Forget her," advised Josh. "She thinks you're a pinhead."

"Dare me, Josh," said Kevin. "Dare me to go over and talk to her."

"I dare you," said Josh with a devious grin.

"Now dare me to ask her out."

Josh laughed, beginning to enjoy the game. "I dare you to!" he said.

Kevin smiled. "Remember," he said, "you dared me." Kevin stood up and prepared himself for the excursion. His clothes looked great, his shoes were tied, his nose was clean, and his armpits were about as fresh as they could be after half a day at school. He was ready.

"What are you gonna do if she says no?"

Kevin grinned a grin as big as all outdoors. "How could she resist a man in shades?" He put his glasses back on. They hugged his ears and nose, no longer slipping off, as if his head had swelled to fit them ... or as if they had sized themselves down to make a perfect match with Kevin's face.

With the glasses firmly stuck on Kevin's face, Josh was quick to catch on.

"Hold it!" said Josh. "Hold it a second. You're

not planning to ... you know ... *use* the glasses on Nicole, are you, Kevin?"

Kevin's all-outdoor smile seemed to wrap itself halfway around his head. "Do you dare me to?"

"No!" said Josh, "I definitely do *not* dare you to!"

Kevin shrugged. "Okay, then, I dare myself."

Josh shook his head. "I liked you better when you were a gutless wonder who got beaten up all the time."

"Aw, c'mon, Josh, if you were me you'd be doing the same thing!"

"No. If I were you," said Josh as he got up to leave, "I'd be scared. Real scared."

Nicole Patterson was part of an eternal trio that also included Iris Beecham and Alexa Macolini. They might as well have been born attached at the hip.

The three of them, like all the other girls in school, were in love with Dash Kaminsky. Kevin imagined that he was all they talked about when they sat down at lunchtime.

Kevin approached and cleared his throat. "Hey, ya wanna see a magic trick?" The three girls turned to him as he approached.

"Not really," said Iris.

"It's a good one ..."

"Does it involve pulling your finger?" asked Alexa.

"No, nothing like that," said Kevin. "I hold in my hand an ordinary . . ." He looked down, then bent to pull up some sod. "An ordinary lump of dirt—but watch closely."

Kevin closed his fist on the dirt. The girls watched, but only because there was nothing better to do.

"I say the magic words," said Kevin. "Abracadabra—"

"Is this lame, or what?" sneered Iris.

"Shut up. This trick needs total concentration."

"Kevin," said Nicole, "I don't know if anyone has told you this, but you are truly weird."

"Abracadabra, hocus pocus, alakazam," said Kevin. "And presto, this clump of dirt is now a diamond."

Kevin opened his palm to reveal a small blue diamond that sparkled coolly in the sun.

The girls stared. "How'd you do that?" asked Alexa.

"I know how he did it," said Nicole. "He tricked us by making us look somewhere else while he switched the dirt for the diamond. It's called misdirection."

"Yeah," said Kevin, closing his fist. "But now the diamond is at the bottom of Iris's Coke. How did it get there?"

Kevin opened his palm and the diamond was gone. Iris shook her Coke and something was, indeed, down there. She guzzled it all the way down until she came up with a diamond between her front teeth. She spit it into her palm and studied it. It was the same diamond.

"Yeah, Nicole, how did it get there?" asked Alexa.

And then, Nicole Patterson uttered a phrase Kevin never believed he'd ever hear her say:

"I don't know."

Kevin smiled and reached behind her ear.

"Another diamond," he said, pulling it out from the strands of her auburn hair. "For you."

He held it out to Nicole with such unashamed sincerity that Iris and Alexa had to break out in wicked laughter. Nicole, now poised on the jagged edge of sheer embarrassment, pushed Kevin's hand away.

"I don't want your dumb diamond," said Nicole. "I just want to know how the other one got into Iris's Coke."

"Yeah," said Alexa, "how did it get there?"

"A magician never tells," said Kevin smugly.

"Hey," said Iris, "he's a magic midget!" The others giggled.

Kevin stiffened and bit his lip, but he refused to be humiliated. Not when he had come this far.

The school bell rang, echoing off the handball court across the field. Kevin was running out of time. If he was going to do something, he'd have to do it soon.

Iris pocketed her diamond. "It's probably plastic, anyhow." And the matter was closed. The girls shoved their sandwich wrappers into their lunch bags and prepared to go inside.

"Wait," said Kevin. "I need to talk to you, Nicole."

"About what?" asked Iris.

"Uh ... It's private."

Iris and Alexa looked at each other and began to snicker.

"Oh!" said Iris. "*That* kind of talk."

"Will you two shut up?" said Nicole.

"No," said Iris. "That's okay, we'll leave you two *alone!*"

"No, wait!" Nicole said desperately, but it was too late. Iris ran off with Alexa, both of them finding this unbearably funny. Nicole turned to Kevin. "Great. You've just ruined my life. Now the whole school is going to think I actually like you."

"Well, don't you like me?" Kevin dared to ask. "I mean ... just a little bit?"

No answer. Kevin tried again.

"Well ... you don't *hate* me, do you?"

"No," Nicole had to admit, "I don't hate you."

Kevin smiled. It was a start. Most of the kids had filtered back into the school. In a few moments they would be completely alone.

"Kevin, this is too weird," said Nicole. "I gotta go." As she turned to leave, Kevin tried to stop her by grabbing her shoulder. Instead, he got his hand tangled in her long hair.

"Ow! Stop it! That hurts!"

"Sorry." This wasn't going as smoothly as Kevin had planned. The second bell rang, and the school's steel doors closed with a heavy echoing thud.

"Listen," said Nicole, "why don't we both just go to class and pretend this never happened, okay?"

"First," said Kevin, "I want you to look me straight in the eye and tell me you don't like me."

Nicole stared straight into Kevin's glasses and said, "Kevin, I . . ."

But Kevin didn't let her finish.

*"You like me!"* said Kevin, and the glasses began to hum. The lenses went dark, and Kevin saw colors swimming in Nicole's eyes. She was frozen, hypnotized; trapped in the invisible web Kevin had spun with his glasses.

*"You like me better than any other boy in school. . . ."* Kevin swore he could see right through her eyes. He could feel his mind spilling through into hers.

*"You want to go out with me more than anything else in the world. . . ."*

Nicole just stood there, unable to speak or move. Kevin could feel the glasses begin to strain. It seemed for an instant that the sun itself dimmed as the glasses pulled in all the energy they could, to move Nicole's mind. A circle of fine frost appeared on the grass around them, and they were surrounded by a pocket of frigid air.

Then it was over. The glasses rested, the cold air blew away, and Kevin, standing alone in the field with a dazed Nicole Patterson, dared to do the unimaginable. He pushed himself up on his tiptoes, leaned forward, and planted on Nicole Patterson's lips the most remarkable kiss on school record.

In spite of the devious, underhanded way Kevin had brought this moment about, his kiss was from the heart. It was the kiss he had always wished he could give Nicole.

When Kevin pulled away, Nicole just stared at him, lost in whatever place it is people get lost in when they've just received such an intensely sincere kiss. But then her lips began to curl, and her eyebrows furrowed. She shivered and blinked, shaking off the spell, snapping out of the trance.

She reached out to grab Kevin's shoulders, and for an instant, he thought she was coming back for more, but instead she pushed him away with superhuman strength.

"Ughhh!" she said. "Ughhh, blaaach blah ugh!" She ran the back of her hand across her lips. "Salami!" she said. "Yuk! Blahhhh!"

She turned on Kevin in such fury, he could only cower from her rage.

"Why, you creep!" she said. "You little troll! You think you can just hypnotize me?"

Kevin was speechless. He kept opening his mouth

to say something, but nothing came out. What went wrong? The glasses were all-powerful, weren't they? Nicole threw her lunch bag at him, and an apple core fell out, bouncing off Kevin's hair. "You can take your dumb plastic diamond and your stupid glasses and your salami kisses and flush them for all I care!"

*You had this coming, you bozo,* said a voice inside Kevin's head. *You deserve this.*

"You're a tiny-minded, tiny-bodied, pinheaded dweeb of a shrimpoid nerd!" Nicole wiped her mouth again.

The pressure on Kevin now was unbearable. All the humiliation, all the rejection. He felt on the verge of some frightening explosion, the way a dwarf star blows up into a supernova.

"You're the shortest, creepiest, dwarfiest little midget on the face of the earth!" shouted Nicole.

Kevin could stand it no longer.

*"OH YEAH?"* he screamed . . .

And that's when Kevin, the dwarf star, went nova.

Mr. Kirkpatrick was out sick that day—down with a cold he had picked up at the Divine Watch.

The substitute was a mealy-looking woman in polyester, whose name was so ridiculously long and unpronounceable she herself had problems trying to spell it when she wrote it on the board. In the end, she advised the students just to call her Ms. Q.

Ms. Q. was trying to rein in the terror when Kevin Midas walked in. The classroom was raging with arguments and spitball wars that showed no signs of stopping.

"Please simmer down," Ms. Q. said to the meltdown situation before her. "I'm taking roll."

Kevin slithered into his seat, and Josh, who sat just across the aisle, watched him. "Kevin, you don't look too good," he said. Kevin imagined that if he took off the glasses, Josh would see in his eyes just how "not good" things were.

Kevin ever so gently put his backpack on his desk.

In the front of the room, Nicole's seat was empty. Josh noticed it right away.

"Where's Nicole?" he asked Kevin.

Kevin didn't know exactly how he should answer that question.

"Kevin," Josh asked again, "what did you do to Nicole?"

"She called me a, midget," said Kevin.

"And?"

"She called me Shrimpoid. . . ."

"And?"

"And I sort of got . . . mad."

*"Where is Nicole?"*

Kevin didn't say anything. Instead he nodded his

head toward his backpack. The light bulb went on in Josh's head.

"No!" said Josh. "You didn't!"

But before Kevin could answer, his backpack was snatched off his desk.

"The ball is in play!" yelled Bertram as Kevin's pack became the prime object hurtling around the room.

"Noooo!" screamed Kevin. If there ever was a time *not* to play keep-away with Kevin's backpack, this was it. Kevin, as pale as the cloud-covered sky, leapt out of his seat in absolute terror.

The backpack flew in the air, and Hal, in the back of the room, caught it.

"I'm giving you five seconds to settle down," said Ms. Q.

Kevin reached Hal, only to watch helplessly as Hal threw the pack to Bertram again. Kevin reached Bertram, and the pack flew again. Bertram laughed and bit down on his gum wad, squirting bubble-gum juice in Kevin's face.

"That's it!" yelled Ms. Q., picking up the phone by the chalkboard. "I'm calling the office." But the joke was on her. The phone hadn't worked since school started.

Bertram grabbed the pack by one thin strap and dangled it out the second-story window.

"You don't know what you're doing!" screamed Kevin.

"C'mon, Midas, come and get it," said Bertram brainlessly. *"Toro, toro!"*

Kevin climbed Bertram's arm as if it were the limb of a tree. Bertram pulled the pack in from the window and prepared to hurl it across the room once more.

What Kevin did next came as a complete surprise, to him as well as to Bertram. He simply had to get that pack back . . . so he hauled off and belted Bertram right in the face.

The pack fell out of Bertram's hands, and Kevin caught it before it hit the ground.

Now the room was a three-ring circus, raging fully out of control. In one corner, a slapping fight had turned into a brawl. In the center ring, a chorus of kids were performing armpit farts, and by the window, Bertram was reeling from Kevin's blow.

Ms. Q. chose to break up the brawl in the corner and drag those two kids out in the hall for a reprimand, leaving the rest of the circus without a ringmaster.

Bertram's lip had been cut against the sharp track of his braces, and his teeth were covered with blood, as if he had just bitten a chunk out of someone. The chain-saw look filled Bertram's face, and Kevin knew there was no escape. He carefully handed Josh his backpack.

"Don't let anyone near her!" said Kevin. The second the backpack was out of his hands, Bertram's foot made contact with Kevin's butt, sending him flying across the room.

"You made me bleed!" yelled Bertram.

Kevin scrambled to his feet, and Bertram stepped on Kevin's toes, firmly pinning his to the ground. "Who do you think you are?" screamed Bertram. "You get a pair of glasses and all of a sudden you think you're king of the world."

He pushed Kevin down, but since his feet were pinned under Bertram's, Kevin came bouncing back like a bobo doll.

"Don't make him mad, Bertram!" warned Josh.

"Why? What's he gonna do?"

Bertram pushed Kevin down over and over again, and Kevin just kept trying to scramble away. He didn't want to fight Bertram—he had better things to do, and this was making him furious! Hadn't the day been screwed up enough?

"I'll teach you to make me bleed!" said Bertram, and with that he spat his gum into his free hand and smeared it across the top of Kevin's head. He kicked Kevin's legs out from under him, and Kevin fell to the floor, his hair impossibly snarled with Bertram's gum.

Bertram laughed. He had won. Just like always.

"You're just a loser, Midas," he said, looking down at Kevin. "That's all you'll ever be, a loser."

With every bit of his body aching, Kevin gritted his teeth in anger and spoke to Bertram with a deadly growl that seemed to climb up from the pit of his stomach.

*"Go to hell, Bertram!"* said Kevin.

And the glasses began to swirl with color.

It all took place so quickly, everyone was caught off guard, and no one was sure what really happened. No one but Kevin, that is, who saw everything in 3-D Technicolor.

The ground beneath Bertram's feet tore open, and flames brighter than lightning leapt out, wrapping around him like tentacles, pulling him downward. There was a far-away hollow sound—a distant chorus of wailing voices that blended with Bertram's wail as he fell. He grabbed for a chair and took the chair with him.

Bertram slipped into the fiery mouth—as it swallowed him whole.

Kevin caught sight of Bertram's eyes as he dropped into the pit. Then Bertram was gone, and the hole that had split open the wooden floor vanished as if it had never existed.

All that was left of Bertram was the echo of a distant cry that soon became nothing more than the moaning of the wind. And then silence.

Everything was exactly the way it was before; the only thing missing was a chair. And Bertram.

It all happened in the blink of an eye, and kids were still turning their heads to see what that flash of light was.

Ms. Q. came running back into the room. "What was that?" she asked.

"*Spontaneous Human Combustion!*" screamed Ralphy Sherman, flapping his arms like a crazy pigeon. "*Spontaneous Human Combustion!!*"

Ms. Q. dragged Ralphy straight to the principal's office.

# CHAPTER 9

# Out of Mind

The rest of the afternoon seemed to unfold around Kevin and Josh like one of their school plays—they were part of the production but hid so far upstage that no one noticed them.

They kept their mouths tightly shut and watched.

At first there was some confusion about Bertram's disappearance in Ms. Q.'s unruly classroom, until someone claimed to have seen Bertram run down the hall.

"Yeah, that's what happened," said someone else, and before long, everyone just figured Bertram had cut class (a common enough occurrence) and he'd turn up eventually. Only Hal protested, but no one ever listened to Hal, and they weren't about to start listening now.

Kevin suffered through the rest of the day with ice-cold, shaking hands and spoke to no one.

"I wish . . . I wish the glasses would stop working," he desperately whispered to himself, hiding alone in a bathroom stall between classes—but the glasses just vibrated and buzzed like feedback through the auditorium microphone, growing hotter and hotter, until Kevin had to fling them from his face. The sleek visor blade had power over everything except itself. Wishing them to stop was about as useless as wishing it had never happened.

Kevin shuffled around for the rest of the day with a pale green face that grew greener every time he thought of Bertram or Nicole—but for the rest of the school, it was business as usual. The bells rang, kids were shuffled around the school like a deck of cards, and eventually both Bertram and Nicole were lost in the shuffle. Forgotten.

*Out of sight, out of mind,* thought Kevin. It was much truer than he could know.

After school, Josh spent a good angry hour blasting Kevin for being such an idiot.

"Bertram deserved to have his head flushed in a toilet, or to be strung up the flagpole by his underwear, but he didn't deserve what you did!" said Josh. "And you should never have tried to control Nicole's mind! I'll bet there's not enough energy in the whole universe to control a mind that stubborn!"

But it was done—and no amount of raving by Josh could undo anything.

A Habitrail rested on Kevin's bedroom desk. He had gotten it for Christmas the year before, but ever since Teri's snake found its way into their mother's jewelry box, animals that could fit in drawers were not allowed in the Midas home, so the Habitrail had never been used.

Kevin supposed his mother wouldn't approve of this, either.

Resting on a pile of cedar chips in the Habitrail was Nicole Patterson, somewhere in the neighborhood of six inches tall.

She was sound asleep—Kevin had put her into a deep sleep the moment he had wished her small, but she was bound to wake up sooner or later.

"Well," said Kevin, "it could be worse; I could have turned her into a shrimp."

"Yeah," said Josh. "I'm sure she'll thank you when she wakes up."

Kevin looked down in shame.

"You oughta use those glasses to wish your lips into a zipper," said Josh, "so you can shut your fool mouth!"

Kevin nodded. "I deserved that."

"Damn right," said Josh. "You deserve a lot worse . . . but I don't know what."

The glasses were now in Kevin's shirt pocket, and he touched them with his right hand, as if pledging allegiance. He longed to put them on and feel their weight on the bridge of his nose. The glasses would take away the shame and the fear. They would make him feel strong and untouchable. Now all he felt was weak and empty. Every time he took those glasses off, they seemed to take a chunk of his soul with them.

At about five o'clock, Nicole woke up.

Kevin and Josh, instantly chickens, dove to the ground and hid, without making as much as a single cluck.

"What the . . . ?" Nicole looked around. "All right, very funny. Now let me out."

Kevin peeked to see Nicole standing on the red running wheel that was normally reserved for small rodents.

"Kevin Midas!" said Nicole, "I should have known it was you. There better not be any hamsters in here!"

"No," said Kevin, "just you."

She yawned. "What time is it?" She looked down at the microscopic Mickey Mouse on her wrist. "Oh no! I missed gymnastics. I'd better get home, or my parents will kill me!"

"But, Nicole . . ." said Josh, climbing out from underneath the desk, ". . . you can't go home in your . . . um, condition."

"What condition?" asked Nicole.

Kevin grimaced. Was she so bewildered that she didn't know what was wrong?

"Nicole," said Kevin, "you may not have noticed this . . . but you're very, *very* small."

"I'm not small, I'm petite," she said. "There's a

big difference. And besides, there are no small people, only small minds."

Nicole hopped off the running wheel and came right up to the plastic wall of the cage. She looked straight into Kevin's right eye, which, to her, must have seemed the size of a classroom globe.

"Joke's over," she said. "I have to get home."

*Something's wrong with this,* thought Kevin. *She's acting . . . well, she's acting like Nicole, not like the victim of a freak miniaturization.*

Kevin looked at Josh, who just shrugged, and so Kevin did as he was asked. He let Nicole out.

"Where's your phone?"

Both Kevin and Josh pointed dumbly to the phone sitting across the desk, and watched as Nicole climbed over a book, nearly losing a shoe in a sticky old soda stain, then climbed the face of the phone and heaved the receiver out of its cradle.

"I don't get it," said Josh. "Is she in shock or something? Doesn't she care that she's been Barbie-fied?"

Nicole went about her business, jumping on the phone buttons to dial them as if she did this every day.

"I don't get it, either," said Kevin.

Nicole knelt by the receiver as her mother answered on the other end.

"Hello?"

"Hi, Mom, it's me," said Nicole in that squeaky, mousey voice.

"Nicole?" said her mother, confused and startled by the strange sound of Nicole's voice. There was silence for a moment, but then Mrs. Patterson's confusion quickly passed away. Too quickly, Kevin thought.

"Thank God you're all right! You had us all worried, little lady—we had no idea where you were."

"I'm at a friend's house," explained Nicole. "I forgot to call."

"We'll talk about it when you get home," said her mother sternly.

Nicole sighed. "I'll be there as soon as I can."

"Good," said her mother. "And watch out for cats on the way home."

Kevin hung up the phone for her. *Cats?* he thought. Did she say *watch out for cats?*

"You see the trouble you got me in? Wasn't your salami kiss bad enough? Now you have to kidnap me, too?"

Josh perked up. "You kissed her?"

There was no time for Kevin to answer, for just then his door sprang open with a bang, and Teri stormed in, unannounced, as she often did.

"Moron police," she said. "All morons present I.D."

Then she stopped dead, coming face-to-face with the Barbie-fied Nicole. Teri's jaw dropped dumbly, making her look like the only actual moron in the room.

Silence hung in the air like the Hindenburg.

Kevin braced for the explosion.

But it didn't happen.

Yes, for a moment terror and confusion filled Teri's eyes, but then Teri blinked, and the terror vanished. It was as though her whole brain had adjusted to accept what she was seeing ... just as Nicole's mom had adjusted to the voice she was hearing over the phone.

"Hi, Nicole," said Teri as if everything in the world was perfectly fine.

Nicole waved. "Hi, Teri. Tell your brother that he's a waste of valuable protoplasm."

"I would, but I think he already knows." Teri sauntered out of the room as quickly as she had entered. "Better hope I don't tell Mom you're hiding a girl in your room." And then Teri disappeared into her own room.

"What is this?" cried Josh. "Has the whole world gone schizo?"

And then the truth swung itself at Kevin with such fury that his brain was launched into deep, deep left field.

He suddenly understood.

Kevin coughed out his wind, and no amount of rapid breathing could bring it back.

"Excuse us, Nicole." He grabbed Josh by the shirt and pulled him out into the hallway, still unable to catch his breath.

"Talk to me, Kev," said Josh. "Don't just stand there like a fish gulping air."

Kevin grabbed Josh by the shoulders and looked him right in the eye.

"Josh, how tall was Nicole yesterday?"

"She was *normal*, Kevin. You remember what normal is, don't you? About three inches taller than you!"

"Okay," said Kevin. "Now close your eyes and try to remember that. Try to remember the last time you saw her looking 'normal.' "

Josh closed his eyes, and after a few moments, his eyebrows wrinkled and knotted. "I can't," said Josh. "I can't picture it."

"Okay," said Kevin. "Now tell me what happened to Bertram."

Josh took a step away from Kevin. He rubbed his arms, as if he were cold. "You sent him to the land down under."

"And what did Bertram look like?"

Josh thought for a moment, and his eyebrows knotted up again.

"Well . . . he had braces. . . ."

"What else?"

Josh stammered a bit.

"What else?"

"Give me a minute. . . ."

"What about his hair, his eyes, how tall was he?"

"I DON'T KNOW! I can't remember, so just shut up about it, okay?"

Josh looked terrified, and Kevin knew why. It was as if someone had yanked something out of their heads. It was like that old trick of pulling a tablecloth out from underneath a perfectly set table. Everything looked fine, but something was missing.

Josh couldn't remember, and neither could Kevin. If he tried really hard, he could remember Bertram's voice, or part of his face, or the smell of his gum, but the memories were fading, becoming harder and harder to find.

"What did you do, Kevin? My God, what did you do?"

"I think . . ." said Kevin, "I think I've changed the rules, somehow."

Josh scowled at him, trying to understand.

"It's like . . . you know, when you're dreaming; first you're in your house, then suddenly you're at school, then suddenly you're at the mall in your underwear, but no one notices—not even you—because while you're dreaming, you don't notice when things don't make sense. You don't notice when the rules change, you know?"

Josh's lips started to quiver. He was breathing fast, too, and Kevin knew that he was beginning to understand.

Kevin slipped the glasses out of his pocket and put them on. His whole body surged with warmth.

"See, Josh, if I were to say something like 'two plus two equals three,' suddenly it would be true, and no one would know any better."

Josh reached out and plucked the glasses from Kevin's face. They made a suction sound as they came off, like a snail being pulled off a window.

"When I first got the glasses, Josh, they just made things—but now that I've had practice, and gotten better at it, the glasses are doing even more. Now the glasses are re-making the rules. They're *re-imagining* the universe!"

They both glanced into Kevin's bedroom, where Nicole was bouncing on an eraser as if it were a miniature trampoline.

"So no one's going to notice anything strange about Nicole being six inches tall?" asked Josh.

"No one . . . they'll just look right past it, and not give it a second thought, like it's normal . . . and it's the same with Bertram. Pretty soon, Bertram's going to be completely gone. No one will remember he ever existed—not even his own parents. . . . Nobody but you and me."

"Why me?" asked Josh. "If *you're* the one changing the rules, how come *I* know something's wrong?" But Josh answered his own question. "It's because I was there with you when you found the glasses, isn't it?"

Kevin nodded. "We're in this together."

Josh looked at the glasses, which were still in

his hands. Kevin's tone changed. "I'd like them back, please," said Kevin.

Josh's grip tightened on the lenses. "Maybe I should keep them for you . . . so there's no more trouble."

Kevin reached out a hand, and his fingers closed around the glasses as well.

"Let go, Josh."

They stood there, facing off—neither of them letting go.

"Jump ball," said Josh, with a nervous chuckle.

"Let go, Josh."

There was something in Kevin's voice— something so commanding that Josh couldn't fight it. Josh let go, and his shoulders sagged. Kevin shoved the glasses back into his shirt pocket, and Josh rubbed his hands on his pants, as if trying to wipe off invisible blood.

"I'm an accessory," said Josh, with bitter resignation. "An accessory to the crime."

Kevin saw Nicole to the door. He offered to walk her home, but she wouldn't allow it.

"I'm fine by myself," said Nicole. "Cats are stupid, anyway."

As she stood on his palm, before Kevin let her down to the ground, she took a long look at him.

"You know," said Nicole, "you should have waited."

"Huh?"

"You should have waited before you kissed me. It was a really dumb thing to do. You should have waited till we were, like, going out or something."

Kevin set her gently down on the sidewalk. "But you'd never go out with me."

Nicole shrugged. "You never asked me." Then she turned and began the long, long walk back to her house four blocks away.

# CHAPTER 10

## Specters in the Dark

Kevin told himself he wouldn't use them again. No matter how miserable he felt without the glasses on his face, he swore he'd stop once and for all.

Yet as he lay in bed that night, thoughts of the glasses pushed everything else out of his aching head. He knew where they were, so close, sitting there in his shirt pocket, hung on the back of his desk chair.

*It wouldn't hurt just to look at them,* thought Kevin, and so he heaved his cold, shaking body out of bed, took the glasses from his shirt, and set them open on his desk.

About a foot away from the wall outlet.

The glasses had already drained the heat from the room, but it wasn't enough. They sat there spent and powerless, just like Kevin, in a room that had become as cold as winter. Now the blade of the lenses was a dull, foggy gray, like cheap plastic that had been washed too many times.

In a moment, an arc of blue electricity bridged the cold air between the glasses and the outlet. It looked like one of those mad scientific devices in old monster movies.

Kevin slipped under his blankets and watched. *It wouldn't hurt to let the glasses charge up just a little,* he thought. Only they didn't charge just a little, they charged a lot. For half an hour Kevin watched and listened to the gently crackling electrical hum while everyone else slept.

Soon the glasses looked perfect again. The smooth visor blade was sharp and shiny—as perfect and pure as a diamond. They sat there, waiting patiently for Kevin.

Now Kevin longed more than ever to have the cold and the emptiness he felt chased away by the glasses.

*If I wore them for just a second, it couldn't hurt,* he thought. Could he bear that? Wearing them for just a second? Of course he could. Then he could put them back in his shirt pocket. That's what he'd do.

He reached out, crooked his finger, and grabbed the glasses, just as he had the first time, when he had seen them on the mountain. He slipped them on his face.

Instantly the icy night rolled over into a thick, warm quilt for Kevin to wrap himself in, protecting him from anything hidden in the shadows.

He stretched and let the warmth relay down his

spinal column until it pulsed in his fingers and toes.

How good it was to feel so warm, so safe, and so comfortable. How could he ever want to feel differently?

Still wearing the glasses, Kevin felt sleep begin to pull him down with caressing hands. He gave no resistance.

Kevin opened his eyes some time later, deep into the night, hearing the distant sound of metal against metal. A rattling sound. A tilt of the head told him that the sound came from the left side of his room—more specifically, his closet.

Kevin sat up and walked what seemed to be twice the usual distance, noticing the sickly-sweet aroma of overripe fruit. Pushed by curiosity, he reached for the knob and turned it. The door creaked open to reveal a place that bore no resemblance to Kevin's closet. And Bertram was there.

Bertram was in the same clothes he wore the moment he was sucked out of the world, only now they were drenched in sweat.

*Yes. Now I remember what he looked like* was the first thought that flashed in Kevin's mind. Then the shock and horror followed it in, like thunder.

Bertram lunged at Kevin in fury, only to be choked back by the chains. Heavy black chains circled his legs, arms, and neck, rattling like iron bones. They were fastened securely to a jagged wall of steaming, black, shiny stone, which had replaced the walls of Kevin's closet. The glass-like obsidian shimmered, reflecting fires unseen.

It was *exactly* what Kevin imagined Hell to be like.

Except for the fish.

Bertram's Hell had fish everywhere. They flopped at his feet, they slithered down the wall and into his shirt. And they all smelled like used fruity bubble gum. It must have been Bertram's worst nightmare.

"You're *dead*, Midas!" screamed Bertram. "You're dead when I catch you! You're gonna pay!"

And then Bertram's face changed. He wasn't a grimacing demon anymore, but a terrified thirteen-year-old boy.

"Please," he whispered desperately, "please, Kevin, help me. I'm scared ... pleeeeeease ..."

"I'm sorry!" cried Kevin. "I didn't mean it! I didn't even know there really *was* a Hell!"

Bertram changed again. His face twisted into a snarl, and he lunged forward like a madman, only to be choked back once more by chains that seemed strong enough to hold a dinosaur.

"You idiot!" growled Bertram. "You *made* this place! You made it for me!"

Kevin knew it was the truth. Whatever other places there might be—in and out of the universe—this particular Hell was invented just for Bertram.

The rage left Bertram's eyes again, and once more he was just a kid. He began to cry. "Please, Kevin, please, I'll be nice to you. I'll be your friend, just please get me out of here. . . ."

*If I step in the closet,* Kevin thought, *if I just cross over, I can bring him back.*

Bertram stretched his hand out as far as he could, and Kevin took one step toward the closet, reaching for Bertram's grimy, wriggling fingers.

Then Bertram turned into an old winter coat, and the rattling chains became nothing more than the wire hangers clattering in the breeze of an open window. Kevin found himself in his pajamas, standing at the closet door.

The dream, and the memory of Bertram's face, were already fading, but still Kevin knew this was no ordinary dream. Not just because of how real it felt, but because of the smell that still filled the house. The awful bubble-gum stench of a million rotten strawberries.

Kevin stood for the longest time in front of Teri's bed, not having the nerve to wake her up. Eventually she awoke by herself, to see Kevin standing there, the way an ax murderer might. She gasped, then angrily threw a pillow at him. "You don't scare me," she declared. "So get outta here."

Kevin didn't move. Teri sniffed the air.

"Ughh! what is that stink? Did you fart, Kevin?"

"No," he answered. "Teri," he said, his voice quavering, "I gotta talk to you."

"Oh, for God's sake, it's three in the morning!"

She peered at him in the darkness. Maybe there was enough light for her to see the trouble painted on his face. He had taken the glasses off, leaving them on his desk again, away from the outlet. He wondered if he looked as weak as he felt. *It's all wrong,* he thought. *I shouldn't have to wear those stupid glasses just to feel good. I used to be able to feel good without them.* But he couldn't even remember what that had been like.

"Is this about Nicole?" asked Teri. "You know she likes you."

Kevin nodded. He knew that now. He had figured out that the glasses didn't control Nicole's mind because they didn't have to—she had already liked him. Of course that didn't mean she had to admit it—not even to herself. But that was screwed up now, too.

"It's about a whole lot of things," said Kevin. "I'm . . . I'm in trouble, Teri."

Teri stared at him, studying him for the longest time.

"Something's really wrong, isn't it?" she whispered.

Kevin nodded.

"Climb aboard." Teri tossed him her favorite pillow, and Kevin hopped onto the end of her bed, sitting with his knees tucked into his chest. True, much of the time Teri was a general nuisance to Kevin, but that was only part of her job as his big sister. This was the other part.

"Tell me," said Teri. "Tell me everything."

"You won't believe me."

But the look on her face said that she would. No matter how crazy or awful his secret was.

"If it's the truth, then I'll know," she said. Then she added, "But if you woke me up in the middle of the night to tell me a lie, I'll beat the crap out of you."

She took his foot in her hands and began rubbing it, to get it warm.

Kevin told her everything, from the beginning, and even though it was the word of her crazy brother against the rest of the sane, rational world, Teri did the most wonderful thing a sister could ever do. She chose to believe her brother.

It was nearly dawn when Kevin was done. Teri didn't say anything. She just sat there, staring at him. Then she finally said, "We have to do some serious thinking."

"Can I stay with you tonight?"

Kevin hadn't asked that since he was six, yet somehow he didn't feel ashamed to ask her now. He didn't think Teri would let him leave, anyway. He doubted she wanted to be alone, either.

"As long as you don't snore," she said, then

changed her mind. "Naah. You can snore as much as you want."

They lay on the bed, stretched out in opposite directions, but neither one of them slept. Soon early dawn washed the room gray, and Kevin could hear his father getting ready for his morning run.

On his way downstairs Patrick Midas passed by Teri's open door, and stopped when he caught sight of Kevin there. Teri pretended to be asleep, but Kevin didn't. He stared right at his father.

Mr. Midas stood on the threshold for a moment, as if he were about to speak. Kevin wanted him to speak—to say anything. *If I told Teri,* thought Kevin, *I could tell him, too. Whether he believed me or not, at least he'd have to do something. Anything.*

Mr. Midas lingered by the door for a moment, then turned away. Kevin could hear him bounding down the stairs and out the door.

"He didn't even ask what I'm doing in here," whispered Kevin. "He knows something's wrong, but he didn't even ask." Kevin couldn't remember the last time either of his parents wanted to know anything. They didn't ask about his recent mood swings, or what he spent his time thinking about. They didn't ask about the bursts of energy and hours of weariness that had filled his life since he found the glasses. They rarely seemed to notice when Kevin was out of whack, and when they did notice, they would write it off as if it were nothing.

"If I were strangling to death, Mom would shove spoons of Robitussin down my throat to make it all better," Kevin told Teri. "If I were drowning, Dad would say, 'No pain, no gain.' They never ask what's really going on. Don't they even care?"

"They care," whispered Teri. "But they won't ask because they're afraid of the answer."

# CHAPTER 11

# Life As We Know It

Kirkpatrick was back in school on Monday, as Josh Wilson had hoped.

Josh had avoided Kevin like the plague all weekend, and on that Monday morning he didn't wait for Kevin to show up at his door. He left early because he needed time to think things through without Kevin. . . . Kevin was getting creepy, and there were things going through Josh's mind that he wouldn't dare share with Kevin, even if he were his best friend.

The fact was, things weren't "right" anymore. Not just the things Kevin had been wishing for, but things in general—things all around. Ever since Kevin had found those glasses, the days had begun to *feel* strange, but Josh couldn't put that feeling into words—or maybe he was just afraid to.

So Josh went to talk to Kirkpatrick. If he could talk to anyone at school about such things, it was Kirkpatrick. He was the only real philosopher among the Ridgeline Middle School teachers—he always seemed to have a keen interest in and an open mind to even the weirdest of notions. Besides, Kirkpatrick had started the whole thing. He was the one who planted the idea of climbing the mountain in Kevin's head, about as powerfully as Bertram had planted the pinecone in Kevin's mouth.

The first bell was still twenty minutes away when Josh arrived in Mr. Kirkpatrick's classroom. Kirkpatrick sat at his desk, with a red, sniffy nose, correcting papers and taking care of all the problems left behind by Ms. Q. He didn't notice Josh until Josh was halfway to the front of the room.

"You're early today, Josh."

"Yeah. Can I talk to you, Mr. Kirkpatrick?"

The teacher put down his pen and papers and looked up as Josh sat down in the closest chair. "Something wrong? Was it Ms. Quaackenbusch? Are other kids giving you a hard time?"

"No, nothing like that," said Josh. He was beginning to understand just what it was he wanted to ask, but how could he come right out and say it?

"Mr. K.," asked Josh, "how do you think the world is going to end?"

Kirkpatrick looked at him for a moment, and laughed. "I was expecting maybe girl trouble," he said. "I mean, don't seventh graders have enough to deal with without thinking about the end of life as we know it?"

He studied Josh and finally realized that Josh was dead serious. Kirkpatrick leaned back and ran his fingers through his uneven hair.

"I don't think the world *will* end, Josh. I don't think it *can*." He glanced up at the humming fluorescent lights and rocked a bit in his chair. "But when I was younger, I used to think about it a lot."

"What did you think about?"

Kirkpatrick shrugged. "A bunch of things. You know, nuclear war—someone turns a key, and poof, everything's gone. Sometimes I would wonder if there was really a great flood thousands of years ago, and if there might be another one. I would think about the dinosaurs and how they might have been wiped out by a meteor striking the earth—and wonder if it could happen again."

Josh felt the tips of his ears begin to tingle as if they were getting cold. There were times when he had thought about these things, too.

"But I don't worry anymore," said Kirkpatrick. "Now I just trust that those things won't happen."

Josh shook his head. "I don't think that's how the world's going to end." He leaned in closer as he spoke. "I think it's going to be a quieter thing. It's going to happen in a way that no one even notices anything is wrong. I think things are going to sort of . . . stop making sense . . . bit by bit. Things won't work right, people won't think right, everything's going to get all mixed up, until nothing in the universe works the way it's supposed to. . . . And then, everything will just . . . stop."

"The Dream Time," said Kirkpatrick, raising his eyebrows.

"The what?"

Kirkpatrick took on that knowing look of a shaman—as he had around the campfire two weekends before. "There are some cultures," he said, "that believe there will come a time when dreams cross the barrier into the real world, and the real world is dragged into an endless dream. All the laws of science and logic will break down into the chaos of nightmares. Pretty wild, huh?"

Josh could feel his hands and feet grow numb. Kirkpatrick didn't know it, but he had hit the nail right on the head. *This* was exactly what Josh had been sensing. Everything was sort of . . . slipping away, and it was all because of Kevin and those awful glasses. Josh wanted to run home and take a shower to wash the feeling away. He wanted to slam his fist against the wall, just so he could feel it and know that it was real and not a dream.

"You think that could happen?" asked Josh. "The Dream Time?"

Kirkpatrick waved his hand as if he were swatting away a fly. "Naah. It's an ancient superstition made up by people who needed to explain things. It's the same as believing the world is flat, or that the sun revolves around the earth."

"But the prophecy," said Josh, practically climbing out of his chair. "The legend about the Divine Watch—those people had to know something!"

Kirkpatrick leaned back and laughed again. "Is that what this is all about, the mountain?"

"The prophecy makes sense!" said Josh.

"Maybe so," said Kirkpatrick, "but I made it up."

Josh backed up until the hard wood of his chair pressed against his shoulder blades. "You what?"

"I made it all up. It was a good campfire story," said Kirkpatrick, a bit pleased with himself. "Too good, I guess."

Josh couldn't look at him now. "You don't understand. . . ." he mumbled.

"Sure I do," said Kirkpatrick kindly.

Josh couldn't let it go. There had to be a way to get through to him. *"Nicole Patterson is six inches tall!"* Josh blurted out.

Kirkpatrick thought about that. "Well . . . I never gave it much thought . . . but now that you mention it, yes, she is about the size of a shoe. So?"

"So, doesn't that seem strange to you?"

"Should it?"

Josh threw his hands up in the air.

Kirkpatrick began to tap his pen against his desk and chew on his upper lip. "Josh, . . . maybe you ought to go down to guidance and have a talk with Dr. Cutler."

"Why?"

"Well, . . . obviously something is troubling you. Maybe she could help."

"I'm not crazy!"

"No one said you were."

Josh stood up so fast the chair flew out behind him and fell to the floor. He headed for the door as quickly as he could, but before he left he turned back to Kirkpatrick.

"One more thing . . ." Josh kept his hand on the doorknob, as if touching something—anything—solid and real would give him the courage to ask the question he needed to ask and face the answer he knew he would get.

"How much," asked Josh, "is two plus two?"

Kirkpatrick looked at him, expecting there to be a punch line. "What's your point, Josh?"

"Just answer the question," said Josh.

Kirkpatrick shrugged. "Three, of course. The answer is three."

# CHAPTER 12

# Don't Touch
# That Dial

Rumor was that Hal Hornbeck lost it completely that same day, during fourth period. Not that Hal had ever been wrapped too tightly to begin with, but for some reason, he walked into his Spanish class and went totally loco. Everyone who saw it had their own version of the story, but everyone did agree on this basic sequence of events: Hal had walked into class, looking tired and confused. Then, for no apparent reason, he launched into a screaming fit and had to be dragged out.

Rumor also had it that he refused to say anything that made sense to Dr. Cutler, the guidance counselor. He just kept asking for Bertram, whoever that was, perhaps an imaginary playmate.

Kevin and Josh, who did not have Spanish class with Hal, heard all of this in passing, but didn't think much of it. They had enough concerns of their own.

Kevin and Josh also avoided Nicole Patterson to

the best of their ability, which might have been a mistake, because Nicole, who *was* in Hal's Spanish class, had the most accurate description of what really happened. Nicole claimed that Hal walked into the room, saw her, and began screaming at the top of his lungs. Everyone thought it was pretty funny that a clod like Hal could be frightened by someone as petite as Nicole.

During lunch, there was further talk about how Hal had gotten a zero on his first-period math quiz, but Kevin was too busy looking for his sister to care much about the current status of Hal Hornbeck's math skills. Kevin was hoping Teri had come up with some advice as to what to do about the glasses.

Teri did, indeed, have some advice.

"Take the glasses, and smash them with a sledgehammer," she said. "I'll do it for you if you want." That was easy for *her* to say—they weren't hers. She wasn't the one who *needed* them. She wasn't the one who got sick when the glasses weren't around.

"They can't be destroyed," said Kevin.

"How do you know? Have you tried?"

"What if we try to destroy them and they destroy us instead, in defense?"

"You're talking like the thing is alive—it's just a pair of glasses."

Kevin didn't answer her, and his silence made Teri shudder. "Then we'll bury them," said Teri, "where no one will ever find them. You, me, and Josh together—okay?"

Kevin squirmed his way out of answering her. If she had made this suggestion the night before, when he was weak and vulnerable, he would have gone out with her in the middle of the night in his pajamas, and buried them halfway to China. But that was then. Now Kevin had a better idea, one that he was certain would work just fine, although he wasn't about to tell anyone. He would keep wearing the glasses, but learn to shut up.

Kevin was reminded of a diabetic kid he knew. The kid went to class, played sports, had fun—was normal in every way. The only thing was, he had to have a shot of insulin every day, for the rest of his life.

That's how it would be with Kevin and the glasses.

*What's the big deal?* Kevin told himself. He had worn glasses every day for as long as he could remember. So now the rest of him needed glasses as much as his eyes did—what was the difference, really? He could grow used to keeping the glasses on and keeping his mouth shut, the way the diabetic boy got used to his insulin shots.

Kevin was thinking about this when suddenly his crystal-clear world became blurry once more.

Kevin didn't see the face of the kid who stole his glasses—but by the shape lumbering down the hall, he could tell who it had to be.

Hal Hornbeck.

Hal didn't taunt Kevin—he didn't play keep-

away, or bullfight, or rodeo. He simply took the
glasses and just kept on running until he burst out
the side door of Ridgeline Middle School 'and disappeared.

Kevin scarfed down a slice of pizza, practically
inhaling it.

"I'm so dumb!" said Kevin. There was no argu-
ment from Josh and Teri, who were sitting across
from him at the pizza parlor. "I should have
known," said Kevin. The fact was, Josh should
have known, too. There were, after all, *four* of
them there when Kevin found the glasses, and now
that Bertram was out of the picture, it left three—
three boys on the outside, looking in on a world
going crazy. No wonder Hal had screamed when
he saw Nicole. They should have known!

It may have taken Hal most of the day to figure
out what was going on, but when he did, he didn't
waste any time. Kevin, Josh, and Teri had immediately taken to the streets to find Hal, but he was in
none of the usual places. He had simply vanished.

"More pizza!" said Kevin.

"You've already eaten an entire pie," complained Teri. "If you don't stop, you're going to
hurl."

"More pizza!" demanded Kevin. He was hungry,
and the more he ate, the hungrier he got. Even
though his stomach was stuffed and he felt like
barfing, he was still hungry.

"Maybe it's better this way," offered Josh.

"Are you kidding me?" said Teri. "Do you really want Hal Hornbeck using those glasses? If you thought Kevin was a screwup, can you imagine what things would be like with *that* pus-head running the show?"

Josh sank in his seat and gnawed on a crust.

Kevin inhaled the last slice on the table, then looked up at Teri and Josh with tired, sunken eyes. "I think I'm going to be sick," said Kevin.

"I'm not surprised," said Josh.

"No," said Kevin, "that's not what I mean. . . ."

Both Teri and Josh were looking at him now, and they were beginning to understand what he meant. The glasses had been gone for just a couple of hours, and already Kevin was looking bad. His eyes were dark, and his skin was pale and pasty. Soon he would start shivering. What came after the shivering? He didn't know, because Kevin had never let it get beyond that—he had always put the glasses back on. But now he couldn't. How bad would the sickness get? How bad *could* it get before . . .

Kevin put down his crust. "Pizza's not going to help, is it?"

They all knew what had to be done.

"Where would you go," asked Teri, "if you were Hal Hornbeck and had a pair of magic glasses?"

When the question was asked in that way, the

answer came quickly and clearly, bringing on a powerful dose of hope.

Hal had done what most kids in town would do under the circumstances. He had gone to the dentist.

Public-access cable took in the video dregs of the universe. Would-be talk-show hosts and local crackpot prophets teetering on the edge of lunacy found a happy home on Channel 92. There were long hours of town council meetings, high school sports recorded on home camcorders, and *really* bad dance recitals. Basically anyone who could afford ten dollars a minute could have his or her own local television show.

Only one local show was watched week after week. "Frankie Philpot's World of Phreakie Phenomena."

The story, as everyone knew, went like this. Frankie, a mild-mannered dentist, had discovered some years ago a set of gold-filled molars that not only picked up a local radio station, but also (when the patient's arms were held up in just the right position) could tune in voices from the great beyond.

From that moment on, Frankie had dedicated all of his nondental time to exploring the supernatural, and he produced his findings at six o'clock every Thursday night.

His dental practice doubled, of course, since every kid in town wanted a paranormal dentist who might be able to tighten his or her braces just enough to pull in radio signals from dead people—or even better—*famous* dead people.

Kids watched his show every week, hoping beyond hope that something mystical would actually happen, but nothing ever did.

This week's show, however, promised to be very interesting.

Kevin, Teri, and Josh arrived at the small office building where Franklin J. Philpot, D.D.S., had his offices. The waiting room was empty when they arrived.

"Dr. Philpot has canceled all his afternoon appointments," the receptionist explained through her little glass window. She handed Kevin a small pink card. "This is a voucher for a free teeth cleaning," she told him. "We're sorry for the inconvenience."

"We don't have an appointment," said Kevin. "We just need to talk to him."

"It's an emergency," added Josh.

"There are *other* dentists," suggested the receptionist, beginning to write them a referral.

"But it's about Elvis!" Teri blurted out.

The receptionist perked up and put down her pen.

"What about Elvis?"

Kevin and Josh turned to Teri. "Yeah, what about Elvis?"

Teri didn't miss a beat. "My retainer," she said.

"Of course I can't be sure, but I've been hearing Elvis singing through my retainer."

The receptionist didn't quite buy it.

Teri pulled the retainer out of her mouth and held it in the receptionist's face. "You wanna check?"

She grimaced and backed away. "Maybe you'd better show Dr. Philpot."

She disappeared into the inner offices, and they snuck in right behind her.

It looked like any normal dental office—several examining rooms with dental couches, X-ray machines, posters about gum disease. The only difference was an office in the back that had been converted into a low-budget television studio.

Hal Hornbeck sat alone in the studio with his feet up, like an emperor, eating chocolates out of a golden bowl.

There was evidence everywhere of Hal's abuse of the glasses—food that must have appeared right before Frankie Philpot's eyes now littered the ground. Philpot was not in sight; he was probably on the phone with someone bigger and more important than himself. This thing was about to blow sky-high, if Kevin didn't do some heavy damage control . . . but he couldn't do that until he got the glasses away from Hal.

"Well, if it isn't the goon patrol," said Hal, not

even bothering to stand up. "I knew you'd get here sooner or later."

"I want my glasses now!" said Kevin.

"Extremely Full Nelson!" said Hal, and instantly Kevin felt his neck pressed forward and his feet lifted from the ground, although no one was there. Kevin couldn't talk—could barely breathe. How dare someone use his own glasses against him!

"It's too late," said Hal. "Philpot's already putting me on this week's show."

"You moron! You can't show the glasses on TV," insisted Teri. "Then everybody will want to take them away!"

Hal gave her an ear-to-ear smirk. "Not if they don't know it's the glasses. Right now Philpot thinks I'm the one with the power, and you'd better not tell him different!"

Just then, Frankie Philpot, dentist of the supernatural, burst into the room, fumbling with his Handycam. His eyes and hair were wild, as if he had just won the lottery. In his excitement it took him a few moments to notice there were new people in the room.

"Are these your friends?" Frankie asked Hal. "Are they . . . like you?"

"No," answered Hal, "they're mere humans."

"Don't listen to him," began Josh. "He's—"

"Josh," said Hal, "you shouldn't talk with a frog in your throat."

Josh suddenly began to gag and cough. Teri

opened her mouth to speak, but when Hal turned to look at her, she shut it again, for fear of what he might do.

Frankie Philpot didn't care about the kids in the corner. He anxiously raised the Handycam, ready to record the magic of Hal Hornbeck.

"I've had this power for as long as I can remember," Hal began, once the camera was rolling. "I was born with it. . . ."

Josh kept trying to clear his throat but couldn't stop gagging. Teri, who was trying desperately to free Kevin from the invisible stranglehold, turned to Josh and gave him the Heimlich maneuver.

"Go on," said Frankie, "tell me everything!" This must have been the highlight of Frankie Philpot's life—documented evidence of a supernatural being. "Where are your people from?" he asked.

"Originally Pittsburgh," answered Hal.

Teri gave a tug on Josh's gut, and Josh coughed out a good-sized bullfrog, which shot across the room like a bullet, right into Hal's face, knocking the glasses to the floor.

"Great aim, Josh!" said Teri.

Kevin flexed his arms and neck, spun around, and finally broke out of the Nelson. He dove to the ground on top of the glasses, like a football player recovering a fumble.

Frankie Philpot did not waver; he had a job to do. "Forget about them," he told Hal, never moving the videocam from his face. "Tell me more about yourself."

Kevin and Josh raced out, and Hal was about to follow, when Teri, thinking quickly, took hold of a dental X-ray machine and pulled on the long mechanical arm that connected it to the wall. The thing looked like a huge blue insect head. She aimed it at Hal's chest.

"Make one more move and I'll fry ·you!" said Teri.

Hal froze in his steps.

At last Frankie lowered his videocam. "Is something wrong?"

Kevin had come to the end of the hallway; all the while his shaking hands fumbled to open the arms of the glasses.

Josh and Teri were on his heels, while, much farther behind, Hal was pursued by Philpot, who refused to let any phenomenon go undocumented. "Wait!" he cried to Hal. "I just have a few more questions."

Kevin turned down a dead-end hallway.

Finally he put on his glasses, and the yellow lettering on the steel doorway ahead of him came into clear focus. It said Danger: High Voltage.

"Kevin, this way!" said Teri as she and Josh turned toward the elevator, at the other end of the hall.

The glasses were already filling ·Kevin with

warmth, taking away his shivers and his headache—but not quickly enough. The electricity was humming behind those doors. Kevin could hear it, and he began to wonder. He pushed the glasses farther up on his face.

All that electricity . . . and only a few feet away . . .

He took a step closer to the steel door of the electrical room, and then another. Josh grabbed his shoulder.

"Don't, Kevin," said Josh, almost reading his mind. "You got the glasses, that's enough. . . . You don't have to do this."

Kevin shook off Josh's arm. "I want to do it." Kevin reached out, pulled open the door, and looked deep into the rat's nest of high-voltage copper coils.

A heavy wave of electricity shot from the transformer and began to course across the surface of the glasses with the random pattern of a tornado funnel. Josh fell to the ground and grabbed firmly onto a steel doorstop, as if he feared being dragged away.

Up above, the lights began to flicker and dim, as if someone in the next room was getting the electric chair.

Teri and Josh had never seen Kevin charge the glasses. It was an awful, private thing they felt they had no business watching, but they couldn't turn their eyes away.

"He'll fry himself!" said Teri. "We have to do something!"

Frankie Philpot and Hal had just turned the corner, and they stopped dead in their tracks when they saw where Kevin had gone.

For Kevin it was like coming to the surface of a deep, cold ocean and taking his first breath. He felt he could breathe in forever and never exhale. It felt better than anything the glasses had ever done for him.

And then something went wrong.

Something cracked.

It sounded like a million chandeliers falling to the ground at once, and it felt like an explosion inside Kevin's brain. He was blown back and went sliding across the floor. The current between Kevin and the transformer died, and the lights returned to their normal brightness.

Teri and Josh helped Kevin up and looked into his rolling eyes.

"Kevin, are you okay?" asked Teri.

"I don't know, I . . ."

"The glasses—they're cracked!" said Josh.

It was true. The glasses had overloaded, and a crack in the left lens was shooting tiny sparks.

"Let's get out of here!"

Josh and Teri practically carried Kevin to the elevator. Hal and Frankie were close behind and made it into the elevator just as the doors closed. Frankie raised his camera.

"I have to get this all on tape!" said, Frankie. "Somebody, please tell me what's going on!"

"You stink, Midas, you know that!" Hal grabbed hold of the glasses and tried to pull them off Kevin's face, but they didn't come.

"Somebody, please say something," begged Frankie. "Anything!"

"Siberia," said Kevin, and he disappeared along with Teri and Josh.

Frankie lowered his camera. "Correct me if I'm wrong," he said, "but did I just witness a transcontinental teleportation?"

"Siberia?" said Hal. "Why would he want to go to Siberia?" Then the elevator bell rang, and the doors opened to the lobby.

Only it wasn't the lobby.

The elevator had opened up to an endless plain of snow, beneath a troubled sky. Before them stood a man with a heavy parka, a funny hat, and a leathery face that peered in at them. Even the yak standing beside him seemed confused.

"Uh-oh," said Hal.

Kevin, Josh, and Teri picked themselves up off the bottom of an empty elevator shaft. The only light came from the cracked glasses, which still sparked like a bad short circuit.

"Take us home, Kevin," said Teri.

He reached up to push the glasses farther up the

bridge of his nose but realized he didn't need to—they clamped onto his head now, in a perfect fit.

Kevin pictured his house, then opened his mouth to wish them home—but they were standing in his living room before he said a single word. He didn't think much of it. Until about a minute later.

# CHAPTER 13

# Haunted House

A black hole, Kevin recalled from his ten-page report on the universe, was a sphere of darkness that swallowed everything that got near it—even light.

His parents often referred to his room as the Black Hole.

A "singularity," Kevin recalled from the same report, was that point in space at the very center of a black hole, where all the laws of time, space, and science ceased to exist.

This was a much more accurate description of Kevin's bedroom on the day the glasses fused onto his face.

It was four o'clock. The sun was still high above the horizon, but Kevin was trying his hardest to fall asleep—to be dead to the world in any way he possibly could. He curled into a ball under his blanket and covered every inch of himself so that he could barely breathe. He tried not to think. Not to think of anything at all.

"I found the wire cutters," said Josh, hurrying into the room. Underneath the covers, Kevin burped, the cracked lens of the glasses sparked, and a pepperoni pizza fell from the heavens, splattering at Teri and Josh's feet.

"Just because all that pizza's coming back on you," said Teri, "you don't have to wish it all over us!"

"Leave me alone." Kevin stirred beneath the blankets, trying not to think of food anymore. He began singing in his head, forcing everything out. *"A-ram-sam-sam, A-ram-sam-sam."* It was the stupidest, most nonsensical song he knew. Words that meant nothing—thoughts that could not possibly take any shape in his mind. *"Goolie-goolie-goolie-goolie-goolie Ram-sam-sam."*

Still, a thought did squeeze its way in. The lens sparked, and an empty glass on his desk began to foam over with root beer.

*Stop thinking!* Kevin ordered himself, but his mind wasn't a light bulb he could just turn off.

When they had returned home from their eventful afternoon, it hadn't taken long for them to discover that they had a new and much more serious problem on their hands.

The cracked glasses had fused onto Kevin's face, and if that wasn't bad enough, the crack was making the glasses malfunction in the worst way.

Now the glasses were having little seizures—backfiring like his mom's old car. The fractured lens would send off a random spark every few moments, and that spark would reach deep into Kevin's mind, dragging whatever he happened to be thinking about into the real world.

He didn't have to wish for it—he didn't even have to want it. He just had to think about it. Controlling what he wished for was hard enough, but controlling his thoughts was like trying to herd a swarm of bumblebees with a goldfish net. The best Kevin could do was create a wall of static in his head and try not to think of things like Godzilla.

The glasses sparked again, and some unseen liquid flushed its way through all the walls of the house. Probably more root beer.

Teri snapped the blanket off Kevin, and Josh approached, holding the wire cutters like a surgical instrument.

"C'mon, Kevin," said Teri. "Now or never."

"No!"

Josh leaned in closer, trying to push Kevin's struggling hands out of the way. "This won't hurt a bit!"

But it would hurt, Kevin knew it. The glasses were as much a part of him now as his eyes or his ears, and as Josh began to squeeze the wire cutters on the left arm of the glasses, Kevin felt a searing pain shoot through his skull. Josh might as well have been yanking out his molars.

Kevin screamed, the lens sparked, and the wire

cutters turned into a rose. The thorns pricked Josh's fingers.

"Ouch!" Josh hurled the rose down into a pile that contained a sponge, a carrot, and a banana, which had originally been pliers, a hammer, and a monkey wrench. "If you don't stop doing that, we won't have any tools left!" complained Josh.

"Stop torturing me!" yelled Kevin. The glasses sparked, and an iron maiden of the Inquisition variety appeared in the corner and clanged to the ground with a deep bell toll. Kevin grabbed his blanket and covered himself head to toe.

"You should be good at shutting off your brain," said Josh. "You've had enough practice."

A Chinese star flew through the air, the four-pointed steel disc just missing Josh's head, and embedded itself deep in the wall.

Josh looked at the weapon and shuddered. "You're really good at getting rid of people you don't like, aren't you?" said Josh. "First Bertram, then Hal ... Am I going to be next, Kevin?"

"I'm sorry," said Kevin, "it was an accident." But even so an apology seemed useless. "We're still friends, right, Josh?"

"Yeah," said Josh, "of course we are." But Josh couldn't look him in the face.

"Kevin, you said you can stop the glasses from working," said Teri. "Tell us how."

Kevin looked away from Josh. "It has to be cold," he said, "dark ..."

"The garage!" said Josh.

Kevin slowly came out from under the blanket. It could work! It might not work for long, but it would buy them time. In the hallway, the extent of Kevin's mental meddling became clearer. It wasn't just the Mona Lisa hanging crooked on the wall, or the roast turkey on the bookshelf, or even the suit of armor by the linen closet that may or may not have contained a medieval knight. Worse were the changes in the house itself. Suddenly angles didn't look right. The floor seemed to slope off, windows weren't quite square, and the walls weren't quite straight. The ceiling seemed farther away, and in the hallway, which somehow seemed longer, there were doors that had never been there before.

It was the type of house Kevin might have passed through in a nightmare.

Teri looked around, troubled. "It's like I'm losing my mind," she said. "I can't remember what's supposed to be here, and what's not."

Kevin knew that as an outsider, Teri could never see things the way he, Josh, and Hal Hornbeck did. If no one told her what was wrong with the picture, it would all seem normal—just as it would to their parents when they got home. Kevin could imagine his mom hanging towels on the armor and his dad carving the turkey for dinner, as if turkeys always appeared on bookshelves for no apparent reason. It was amazing how normal the world could seem to others, when, through Kevin's eyes, it was so incredibly screwed up.

"Trust me," said Kevin, "*none* of it is supposed to be here."

They climbed down the not-quite-straight stairs, opened the not-quite-rectangular door to the garage, and stepped in.

The garage had taken on the same dreamlike quality as the rest of the house. The ceiling seemed to disappear into darkness; the cinder-block walls were damp and covered with mildew. The air was stagnant, like the inside of a tomb, and in the corner, the boiler had begun to take the shape of a face, with the fiery mouth of an iron monster.

The glasses sparked once, and *whack!* a door that had never been there before appeared against the far wall.

"What's on the other side of the door?" asked Josh.

"Disneyland," said Kevin with a sigh.

No one felt like checking.

"Drain the glasses, Kevin," said Teri. "Do it now."

With the simplest thought, Kevin snuffed out the gas fire beneath the boiler, and blew out the single light bulb against the wall. Weeds sprouted up, blocking out the light pouring in around the big garage door. They sat down in a tight circle in the middle of the room.

"Mom will be home soon," said Teri.

"Shh," said Kevin. "This won't take very long." The temperature in the room was already dropping. The glasses still sparked every few seconds, like a slow strobe light, and in the darkness around them objects splat and clanged and fluttered by with each spark. No one moved. No one wanted to know what miscreations—animal, mineral, or vegetable—haunted the house around them.

"Know any good ghost stories?" said Teri.

"Don't even . . ." warned Kevin.

Fifteen minutes later the room was in a deep freeze. Kevin could hear Josh and Teri's teeth chattering along with his own—but it was working. Now the glasses sparked only once or twice a minute.

Kevin's arms and legs felt lifeless, as if they were nothing more than bones with a faint memory of muscle. His joints ached, his head throbbed, and he wondered if he'd have to feel this way forever just to keep the world safe and sane. How long would he last? He wished he could see a future for himself, in a time long after he had escaped from this trap, but he couldn't see any future for himself at all.

A spark lit Josh's face. His skin seemed almost purple in that unearthly light, and Kevin began to wonder if he had, in fact, turned Josh purple. He felt fairly certain that he hadn't.

Josh spoke and when he did, his voice surprised everyone. It seemed hollow and airy, as if they were in an immense cavern, rather than a two-car garage.

"You know how we sometimes sit and talk about time travel and spaceships and the universe and stuff?" said Josh.

Kevin remembered those talks well. Every once in a while, when the mood was right, they would sit in Kevin's darkened room and freak each other out with really Big thoughts—all those wild impossibilities that came teasingly close to making sense.

"You mean you two actually talk about something other than girls and baseball cards?" said Teri.

"Sometimes," said Kevin, his voice weak and wispy.

Josh explained. "Like, what if the whole universe is actually a single atom in someone's fingernail, in another really gigantic universe? And, when you beam up to the Starship Enterprise, what happens to your soul and stuff? And, what if, when you die, you live your life all over again, only backwards?"

"Wow, really deep," said Teri. "I think you guys are retarded."

"Remember this one, Kev?" said Josh. "What if the whole universe is like just a single thought in God's mind?"

"Yeah, so?"

"Well," said Josh, "I think maybe you stole his

thought ... maybe now we're all inside *your* head instead."

The glasses had stopped sparking now. Kevin's strength was completely gone.

"I'm not God," croaked Kevin.

"No," said Josh, "you're not."

The glasses never did run down enough to stop working entirely. Perhaps they drew on radio waves and microwaves and who knew what other forms of energy that zipped invisibly through the air. The glasses were, however, too weak to spark those orphaned thoughts out of Kevin's mind.

With what little energy remained in the glasses, Kevin imagined a barge out in the middle of the ocean; then he imagined all the things he had created onto the barge. Finally, he imagined the barge torpedoed and sinking to the bottom of the sea. When the waves in his mind were clear of debris, he knew it had been done. All of the objects he had dreamt up were gone from the house—but he couldn't change everything. The mysterious doors were still there. The listing walls and crooked ceilings had not returned to normal.

In his bedroom, feeling like death's poorer cousin, Kevin curled up tight beneath his blanket. Josh kept him company. "You know, Josh, the worst part is that I don't even get into trouble for it," he croaked. "At least I could get grounded, or suspended or anything . . . but no one knows what awful things I've done."

"*I* know," whispered Josh.

Downstairs, the garage door ground into action as Kevin's mom returned home from work. His father would be home soon, too, but Kevin would be in a deep sleep that would, if he were lucky, take him to the far ends of the universe and let him stay there a long while.

Teri would cover for him, making up some completely reasonable story to explain why her brother was sleeping at five in the afternoon. His parents would believe it, or at least accept it—in any case, they wouldn't challenge it. His mom would feel his forehead and worry about the flu season. His father would promise to talk to Kevin about his strange sleeping habits, but by the morning, assuming Kevin acted halfway normal, his father would forget.

*They don't ask because they're afraid of the answer.*

Kevin felt the icy talons of sleep drag him down into a numb, dreamless slumber.

Josh got barely a moment's rest that night. He had no way of knowing whether Kevin's glasses would begin to spark again. If they did, not even Josh's bedroom would be safe from Kevin's creations. The rules had changed; the only limit to what *could* happen was the limit of Kevin Midas's overactive imagination. Anyone could be a victim now.

Before they had climbed the mountain, Josh had always prided himself on never giving in to fear— but now it seemed he was afraid of everything; shadows, noises—and worst of all, he was afraid of that awful feeling he would have when he woke up, of not *really* waking up at all—of waking up in what Mr. Kirkpatrick called "The Dream Time."

He had, once more, the urge to smash his fist against the wall, just so that he could feel real, normal pain in his knuckles. But now he was terrified to do even that ... because what if he hit the wall and it turned out to be made of green cheese instead of plaster? *Anything was possible* as long as Kevin was stuck to those glasses, *anything*—from Santa Claus coming down the chimney to a child-eating monster hiding in his bedroom closet. How could he sleep? How could he ever close his eyes again?

"You're losing it, Bro," Josh told himself. "This must be what it feels like to go completely psycho."

Josh kept his vigil until the first rays of dawn, when he finally gave in to sleep.

# CHAPTER 14

# *The Chariot of Helios*

Kevin was hauled out of sleep by his alarm clock at seven in the morning. Even before opening his eyes, he knew that the glasses had begun to charge. They were feeding on the sunlight that was shining through his window and hitting his face. The crippling weakness he felt the night before was already gone, and when he opened his eyes, all seemed right with the world.

The crack on the left lens was actually healing itself. It was only half its original length, and from what Kevin could tell, it had stopped sparking.

He timidly swung out of bed and dressed, every moment expecting sparks to fly from the lens, but they did not come. By the time he went downstairs, he was actually beginning to believe that the worst could be over.

His father, already back from his morning run, was cooking breakfast today, which must have meant he was celebrating the most recent pound he lost.

"I had a craving for waffles and whipped cream," he said.

"Lucky us," said Kevin's mom.

Teri had already scarfed her first one down and was waiting for a second. The moment Kevin came into the room, she eyed him like a hawk.

"Feeling okay, Kev?" she asked.

"Couldn't be better."

"Early to bed and early to rise," said Mr. Midas. "A good night's sleep never hurt anyone." He dropped a waffle on Kevin's plate and squirted it full of whipped cream. "You must have been wiped out."

"You could say that," said Kevin.

"I like your glasses," commented Kevin's mom. "They're very sharp."

"I can't stand them," mumbled Teri. "I wish they would shrivel up and die."

"Teri," said Mrs. Midas, "if you don't have anything nice to say, then stuff your face." She plopped the remainder of her waffle on Teri's empty plate, then got up to clean the eggshell-and-Bisquick mess Mr. Midas had artfully created. She turned on the radio above the sink, and revolting Muzak filled the room. Mrs. Midas claimed that this sort of music helped her window-box cuttings grow.

Currently it was winding down an unnatural violin version of "No Money Down, Deadman," one of Teri's favorite heavy-metal songs.

"I'm going to be sick," commented Teri, as she did every time her mother turned the station on.

For a moment, Kevin was able to forget his troubles, and he smiled a big whipped cream grin. These dumb family mornings were something he had never appreciated before.

"It's good to be back to normal," said Kevin.

On the radio, the song changed to a flowery choral version of "Sunrise, Sunset." Mom sang along, and that was always bad news, because Mom never remembered the words quite right.

" 'Sunrise, sunset,' " mumbled Mom. " 'Sunrise, sunset, quickly, day by day . . .' "

"Normal? There's nothing normal about this family," remarked Teri. "With or without your glasses, this place is a nuthouse."

Mr. Midas sat down with an oversized waffle and made it disappear beneath a mountain of whipped cream, while Mom continued to sing.

" 'One season da-de-da de dum-dum, lifetimes of happiness, my dear . . .' "

And then the morning was shattered by a single thought—one spark that sprang from the hairline fracture in Kevin's glasses.

Teri saw the spark and put her fork down.

"Kevin?"

Kevin sat, frozen, the color slipping from his face. "Oh no."

"'Sunrise, sunset . . .'" their mother continued to hum.

"What did you do, Kevin? *What were you thinking about?*"

Kevin swallowed. "The song," he said. "I was thinking about the song."

"No! You didn't! Tell me that you didn't, Kevin! *Tell me!*"

Mr. Midas looked up from his plate. "Something wrong?"

That's when Kevin's whole world went mad. The glasses, which had been gradually building up energy all morning, had finally begun to spark once more, with wild and random bursts.

"Kevin, your eyes!" shouted his mother.

His father reached up and tried to pull the glasses off, only to find that they were no longer a fashion accessory. They were a part of his son.

"Kevin!" He screamed, terrified, and light-years away from understanding. "Kevin, what have you done to yourself?"

"No!" Kevin covered his eyes, and felt the sparks numbing his palms and twisting the world around him. With a spark, their radio was gone, thought out of existence as if it had been nothing more than a daydream. Another spark, and the radio station itself could not be found on any radio dial. Anywhere.

Kevin bolted for the stairs.

"Kevin!" His parents followed.

Teri stayed. She stood slowly and peered out the window, the chorus of the old tune still playing in her head. The sun hung just above the electrical tower on the hill, and it was slowly, slowly sinking into the eastern sky.

*What was wrong with that?* thought Teri. *Was there something unusual about the sun setting at seven-thirty in the morning? Was there? Had it ever been any different?* And Teri began to cry because she could not remember.

Kevin had scrambled upstairs with his panicking parents behind him. He raced down the abnormally long hall.

At the top of the stairs Mr. Midas paused for a split second. *The doors,* said a thought far in the back of his mind. *Since when did this hallway have so many doors?* He hesitated just long enough for Kevin to get to the bathroom and lock himself in.

In an instant, Kevin imagined the bathroom sealed off from the rest of the world as best he could. The window was blocked in with bricks and thick mortar, the bathroom door was welded to the frame in a searing flash of orange light. The vanity lights around the mirror blew out one by one, leaving the small room in darkness.

Kevin didn't have a plan yet, but he knew instinctively what he had to do. Weakening the glasses was not enough. He had to starve them. Starve them until they crumbled and faded out of existence.

"Call a doctor—the police—the fire department," raved his mother.

Kevin's father pounded on the door, begging to be let in.

"Whatever it is, Kevin, we'll help you! Please, son, talk to me!"

Talk to him? What was there to talk about now? Kevin felt a hot and heavy fury that flew out in all directions. Where had his dad been for the past two weeks? Where had he been for the past two years? How could he hope to instantly bridge a gap that had been growing this long?

All the pounding and whining at the door was too little too late—another one of his father's favorite expressions.

A thick tongue of electricity licked out from the outlet across the room and into the glasses. "No!" screamed Kevin, and the force from that single thought fought the electricity back, sending a surge through the wires that melted the circuit breakers and blew out the power throughout the house.

"My God, he's being electrocuted," cried his mom, sounding so helpless that Kevin could almost laugh.

"That's it, I'm breaking down the door!" Mr. Midas began to ram his shoulder against the door as hard as he could.

"Dad, don't!"

He rammed the door again. It bowed inward, but didn't give.

"Dad, please!"

He rammed the door again and again. Kevin cringed in the corner, putting his hands over his ears, and screamed.

*"Stop it! Just leave me alone! Go away!"*

The ramming stopped, and so did the yelling.

The silence that fell was so unnatural Kevin thought he had somehow wished away his sense of hearing. Then, in a moment, when his ears adjusted, he heard the ticking of the clock way downstairs.

"Mom? Dad?" No answer. The boulder Kevin had been feeling in the pit of his stomach rose until he could feel it in his throat.

*Away.*

He had sent them *away.* Not to Siberia, not to a barge in the ocean, not to any place they could ever return from. Just . . . away.

"Mom? Dad? . . . Teri? But his only answer was the ticking of the clock.

When Josh awoke, it was still dawn . . . and yet the clock read 8:00. He had been asleep for two hours, but the sun seemed no higher in the sky. He knew he was awake but kept having to slap his face to get rid of that god-awful dreamy feeling . . . and why was the sky so dark?

Downstairs his mother was cooking.

"You slept late today," she said as he stepped into the kitchen. "Wash up, dinner's almost ready."

At first he thought he hadn't heard her right—but he had.

The scene in the kitchen was too bizarre for words. It was eight in the morning, and his mother, only half dressed for work, was broiling lamb chops.

Then, as if that didn't beat all, Josh's father, who had left for his office over an hour ago, returned home.

"How was your day?" asked Josh's mom.

"Short," said his dad. "Real short."

Josh just watched with a sort of mummified amazement. His mother took off her heels, probably not even realizing that she hadn't been in to work yet, and Josh looked outside again, noticing that the morning had gotten even darker.

*The sun's moving backwards!* thought Josh. *Not just that, but people have suddenly decided that it's evening instead of morning.* He could picture people turning around on their way to work or school and returning home, not even batting an eye.

But it couldn't be! The sun can't just change directions—the Earth can't just start spinning the other way. Such a change would cause earthquakes and mass destruction.

But those were the *old* rules, weren't they—and the old rules didn't count anymore. The world might as well be flat, and the sun might as well be on the back of a chariot that pulled it across the sky ... because it was eight in the morning, and the sun was setting in the east.

Josh skipped his early dinner and paid an emergency call on Kevin Midas.

# CHAPTER 15

# The Keeper of Dreams

It was already dark when Josh reached Kevin's house, and no lights were on. He rang the bell but didn't hear it ring. He knocked but no one answered.

*There's no reason to panic,* Josh said to himself, not believing it in the least.

He climbed in through an open window and quickly discovered that the house had no electricity.

"Kevin? . . . Teri? . . . Mr. and Mrs. Midas? . . ." No answer. The close-cut curls on his head seemed to clench tighter.

He followed the smell of smoke to the kitchen, where a waffle iron was burning over a full gas flame. Josh turned off the burner.

"Kevin, where are you?"

He listened, and after a few moments he thought he heard a weak voice. "Kevin, is that you?"

"I'm up here, Josh," whispered the voice.

Josh climbed the stairs into darkness.

At the top of the stairs Josh saw, at the end of the dimly lit upstairs hallway, the bathroom door.

At first Josh couldn't tell what was wrong with it, but as he drew closer, he could see that a sheet of frost had gathered at the bottom of the door. He could hear something dragging itself across the floor on the other side.

"Kevin, are you in there?"

"I starved the glasses, Josh," came that god-awful whisper. "I did it. They don't work at all now, but I can't get out ..."

As Josh got closer he could see that the door it-self was no longer made of wood. It was a dark, heavy gray slab, and when Josh touched it, his fin-gers stuck to the frozen surface, as they did when he touched the inside of his freezer at home.

The door had turned to lead. Kevin must have lined the entire room to keep all forms of energy out.

"Where's Teri, Kevin? Where are your parents?"

"Away ..." said Kevin. "Just ... away ..."

Josh didn't like the sound of his answer. Bertram had been sent away, too. "Why is the sun setting, Kevin?"

"Never mind that," snapped the raspy voice. "I can't get out. . . . You have to find someone who can get me out ... the police ... firemen ... any-body!" he said. "Because ... I think ... I think I'm dying, Josh."

Josh took a step away. The possibility had never

been discussed, but Josh had feared it all along. That Kevin would abuse those glasses ... until they killed him.

"You gotta help me, Josh ..."

He should have taken the glasses away from Kevin as soon as he knew what they could do. He should have buried them at the base of the Divine Watch, so deep that no one would ever find them. But he hadn't, and now everything had come around full circle, back to him. Josh held the solution to the whole problem in his hands like a heavy, dark sword.

"Kevin, ... if I let you out now, the glasses will start working again ... things will keep changing ..."

"We'll worry about it later," hissed Kevin. "Save me, Josh."

Josh tightened his hands into fists to stop them from shaking. He banged his head against the wall, hoping to knock some sense into it, or at least to knock himself out so he could lose himself in his own dream world instead of Kevin's.

"Josh, are you there?"

There were two truths on the edges of Josh's sword. The first truth was that the only way to save the world was to remove Kevin Midas from it. The other truth was that he loved Kevin like a brother. Tears exploded from Josh's face, and he squeezed his eyes shut to hold them in.

"Josh, why won't you answer me?"

Josh could never win this one. If the solution was like a sword in his hand, then no matter which edge he used, the other edge would cut him down as well. Whether he saved Kevin or the world, he would have to suffer with his decision all of his life. With two choices each worse than the other, Josh knew which one he had to choose.

"Josh?"

"I'm here, Kevin."

"Are you getting help?"

"I . . . I just called the police," said Josh, pushing out the lie like a bad piece of meat. "They're on their way."

"Good." Kevin breathed a shivering sigh of relief. "Thank you, Josh. You're the best friend ever."

Josh pressed his palm against the frozen door once more, losing his battle to hold back the tears. He hadn't called the police. He hadn't called anyone. "Good-bye, Kevin," he whispered so softly that only he could hear it. Then he turned and left.

Halfway down the stairs he began to run and didn't stop running until he got home, where he buried his head deep in his pillow so no one could hear him scream.

In the chill of the October morning-turned-evening, the wind that had spent weeks shattering dry leaves on the pavement stopped dead, hushing like the surf before a tidal wave. The cloud cover that had been spreading out steadily from the Divine Watch for two weeks had, at last, reached the town of Ridgeline.

Single drops of rain began to fall, dampening the ground and preparing it for a sheet of rain, still ten miles away, that rolled south like a wall of water.

In his tiny dungeon of a bathroom, Kevin lost all track of time. He drifted half conscious through the loneliest, emptiest expanses of his mind; a dim universe growing dimmer by the minute. Then for a moment, perhaps the moment before dying, Kevin regained his senses and realized where he was.

It was much later now. Kevin could tell that it had been a long time since he heard from Josh.

"Josh!" he tried to yell, but all that came out was a wheeze of air. He pounded on the door, and it rang out with dull leaden thuds, but no one was out there.

If he closed his eyes now, he knew it would be for the last time.

*But wasn't this what I wanted?* thought Kevin. *To kill the glasses at all costs?*

Maybe not.

There was something he wanted more than that. He wanted to live. Kevin hadn't known that his will to survive could be so strong—so overpowering that it turned his fear into fury. All that mattered was getting out and getting warm—and both those things required giving the glasses whatever they needed.

There had to be a way out—but how? Wishing wouldn't make it so; the glasses were powerless now—and he had sealed himself in there so well it would take a battering ram to get him out. If he were going to live, then the answer had to come from him, and it had to come now.

Then all at once, the answer *did* come.

It was so simple, so amazingly simple, Kevin couldn't believe that it had taken him so long to think of it.

Kevin dragged himself across the icy floor to the bathtub, and with frozen fingers that could barely move, he turned on the hot-water faucet.

The frozen pipes clanged as the water tried to force its way through. Kevin thought it would never come, but finally cold water began to pour into the tub. Degree by degree the water slowly grew warmer until it was scalding hot. It flowed from the faucet, bubbling with heat; filled with energy.

In the dark, Kevin kept his distance as the bathtub filled, so the glasses wouldn't begin working too soon. Then, when the tub was full, Kevin stared at the dark door with a look of sheer determination. He focused all his thoughts on getting out of that awful room . . . and then he touched his fingertips to the surface of the water.

Josh heard the explosion five blocks away, and he instinctively knew it was Kevin. He flew out of the house, sprinting down the street at top speed toward the wall of rain clouds that loomed over the edge of town. He charged through backyards and crashed through hedges on the shortest route to Kevin's place.

He could see from halfway down the block that the front door of Kevin's house had been blown off its hinges by the force of the explosion. Shards of glass from the broken windows lay in the street. Josh raced inside and took the stairs three at a time.

"Kevin!" he screamed. "Kevin, where are you?"

All that was left of the upstairs bathroom was a gaping hole. That, and a bathtub full of solid ice.

"KEVIN!"

Through the huge hole in the wall, Josh could see the backyard, the brush-covered hill beyond, and the massive electrical tower that stood atop the hill like a giant Christmas tree.

That was where Josh spotted Kevin. He was climbing the hill toward the tower—the tower that brought in Ridgeline's entire energy supply.

As soon as Kevin's eyes had adjusted to the faint light after the explosion, he had begun his search for energy. The heat from the water had not been enough; he was still hungry, still cold. The glasses would fix him, but only if they had the energy.

When he saw the tower up on the hill, he licked his lips. Such a tremendous source of power was the perfect place to feed himself and the glasses.

As far as Kevin was concerned, it was the most beautiful thing he had ever seen.

Halfway to the top of the hill, he heard Josh behind him.

"Kevin!" Josh screamed. "No!"

Kevin doubled his speed, scrambling through nettles that scraped his arms and legs. No one was going to stop him from reaching the top. He was going to get there. He *had* to.

"Kevin!" Josh screamed again, closer now. Kevin didn't turn around. He could already hear the electricity humming through the wires.

The nettles thinned to a bald spot atop the hill, out of which sprouted the four legs of the great steel beast. Kevin, unable to catch his breath, now dragged himself between two of the tower's legs, as if crossing through the gates of heaven.

But a demon had grabbed his leg, holding him back.

"I can't let you do it," Josh yelled over the electrical whine, locking himself around Kevin's legs like a ball and chain. "I won't let you!"

Kevin kicked and struggled. "Get your hands off me!" he screamed. Kevin then reached his hand out and pulled a pinecone out of thin air. "You're not my friend!" said Kevin. "A friend wouldn't have left me like that!" He brought his hand down, forcing the entire thing into Josh's mouth, as Bertram had done to him two weeks before.

Josh squealed a muffled cry of pain and loosened his grip just enough for Kevin to kick him away and scramble toward the nearest leg of the tower. The electricity was buzzing in Kevin's ears like a thousand sirens, promising him the world.

Josh plucked the pinecone from his mouth. "Kevin!"

"If you come any closer, I'll turn you into a snail—I swear I will!"

Kevin turned from Josh and reached for the tower.

"If you do it, it'll be the end of everything," yelled Josh, "and you won't be able to blame that on the glasses—because *you'll* be the one who did it! . . . And then you'll be worse off than Bertram!"

"I don't care," Kevin growled. Then he added, "I already am." And with that Kevin firmly clasped the ridge of the girder.

Electricity instantly shot down the tower and surged into the glasses. The rush was more than Kevin could have imagined. He could feel his body and spirit inflate like a balloon. The glasses lapped up the energy, focused it, and sent it surging deep into Kevin's mind. He had never felt so completely energized—he never knew it was possible.

Then something went wrong. The joy became so intense that it began to burn, and the glasses, unable to bear the overload, started to crack again. Hairline fractures like the spiderweb of a smashed windshield spread across the whole surface of the sleek glass blade.

* * *

Josh, just ten feet away, lay on the ground, shielding his eyes. He looked up when he heard the crackling, popping sound of the glasses as they fractured—but still, the current of electricity fed them. Then at last the wires supplying the tower snapped, and with an earthshaking shudder, the arms of the tower melted down into twisted black stubs. The city below was plunged into darkness, and the power supplying the glasses finally died.

Josh could see Kevin now, standing on the scorched ground, looking more like a light bulb than a thirteen-year-old boy. Kevin's whole body seemed bloated, as if he had swallowed an entire ocean.

*My God,* thought Josh, *all that power is still inside of him.* But it couldn't stay in there for long. Josh knew what was about to happen, but all he could do was watch as Kevin Midas became the gateway to the Dream Time.

When Kevin could no longer hold in his ocean of energy, his mind exploded, blowing out through the fractured lens like a fiery supernova.

Josh saw shock waves of change radiate out from where Kevin stood, colorful surges like the northern lights that twisted space and time. Day changed to night changed to day, over and over; stars seemed to swarm in the sky like fireflies, changing their positions in the heavens.

It was like witnessing the creation itself, glorious and horrifying. The birth of Kevin's universe.

In the valley beneath them, space stretched and rippled until it tore open, and from the breach were born creatures of splendor and terror, angels and demons escaping haphazardly out of Kevin's imagination. It all seemed somehow familiar, all these miscreations from Kevin's mind—things Kevin must have seen in movies or comic books. Josh could even swear he saw Godzilla stomping by on the horizon. *My God,* thought Josh, *are these the things that go on inside your mind, Kevin? How could you live with them? How could you stay sane?* But even as the thought occurred to him, Josh knew that the insides of his own mind must have looked pretty much the same. *If I had gotten to the mountaintop first,* he thought, *I could be the one trapped on the other side of those glasses now.* He didn't know which was worse, being the dreamer or being the dream.

If there would ever be rules again—if the world was ever going to be pulled back out of Kevin's mind—then the glasses had to be destroyed now. So Josh leapt into the center of the chaos, right into the eyes of Kevin Midas.

Josh threw his hands before him, grabbed on to the glasses, and the moment he began to pull, he felt something happen to him. What he had feared—what he had sensed from the very beginning was happening! The glasses were pulling him in! Josh felt himself withering—collapsing in upon himself until the glasses seemed to loom like an immense wall of glass.

"Kevin, no!" But Kevin had no control.

With nothing to grab on to, Josh fell through the glasses as they were made of water rather than glass, and he screamed as he plunged down to the crushing core of Kevin's mind, where he would become nothing more than a figment of Kevin's imagination and be blotted out forever.

Josh screamed a single thought as he fell into Kevin's mind. "Break!" he cried to the glasses, praying that, for once, his wish would be stronger than Kevin's.

And then, a moment later, Josh Wilson ceased to exist.

Deep in his mind, Kevin felt Josh's wish ringing in his head. Then he felt the moment when Josh was gone, and the agony was too much to bear.

"Stop!" Kevin wailed, just as the glasses split in half and blew off his face. The force of the explosion threw him to the ground.

His head was spinning as if he had just leapt from the Vomit Wheel at the amusement park. Everything was peaceful and calm. No wind, no sound. Nothing.

"I'm dead," thought Kevin. "I have to be."

When he dared to open his eyes, he knew the

glasses were truly gone from his face, for everything was fuzzy and out of focus.

What Kevin could see of the town below was not a pretty sight. It was still there, but it looked distorted, as if it had been squeezed through a funhouse mirror. It was not daytime, nor nighttime, but both at once. Through dense clouds of many colors, Kevin swore he made out not one but three different sources of light, as if the sun had multiplied itself.

And nothing was moving.

As once before, the silence that filled the air around him was unnatural.

"Josh?" he called, hoping beyond hope that he would be there. He wasn't.

Fragments of the shattered glasses were strewn everywhere, the powerful lenses useless at last. Kevin listened for a sound, any sound that would break the stillness, but there was nothing.

And then it occurred to him what his last command to the glasses had been.

*Oh no! Of all the stupid, moronic, idiotic things I could wish for, this was the worst.*

Just before the glasses had exploded from his face, Kevin had yelled, *"Stop!"* and they had obeyed their final order. The glasses had put the emergency brakes on, stopping time in its tracks, and freezing everything forever like a snapshot.

Everything, that is, except for Kevin Midas.

# CHAPTER 16

## 9:42

Nothing moved.

Leaves and bits of paper that had been spinning in the wind now hung in the air, and gravity was too lazy to pull them down. They stirred slightly as Kevin brushed past, but otherwise they had no more reason to move than all those clocks frozen at forty-two minutes past the hour.

The air was scentless and flavorless as Kevin toured his neighborhood. The people he came across were fixed in their places like mannequins, with eyes open but unseeing, hearts frozen between beats.

All this belonged to Kevin now: a kingdom stretching out in all directions, with no one to threaten Kevin's dominion. Yet as he strolled through the wealthiest mansions in town, he knew there was nothing to be found here that he really wanted. It had been that way ever since his first experiments with the glasses. It seemed the more he had, the more he felt was missing, and now that he had everything, he felt as if he had nothing. An overwhelming sense of emptiness cried out from inside him. *I need ... I need ...*, but he didn't know what he needed anymore.

The sickness had already begun to come on— that sickness of *need* that always took over when the glasses were off his face.

By the time he reached his house, it was already turning him inside out. His head pounded like never before, his temperature was climbing, his teeth already ached from chattering, and if anything had been in his stomach, it wouldn't have stayed there very long. Kevin lay down upon his bed, and as he did, a vision came to him like a mirage in a parched desert.

*The glasses were already healing.*

They had exploded, but the pieces were already drawing themselves together on the top of that hill—for they could be disabled, but never, never destroyed. Even as he thought it, Kevin knew it to be true.

*If you went back up the hill,* Kevin told himself, *and held the shattered fragments in your hand, they would come together right there before your eyes, and then you could put them on.* Perhaps they couldn't set time back in motion again, undoing what Kevin had done, but they could do many more wonderful things that would ease Kevin's lonely existence. Most of all, they would take away the sickness. They would take away the *need*.

But Kevin clamped down his chattering teeth and uttered a single word to his empty room.

"No!" he said.

He would honor Josh's memory. He would resist the powerful pull.

*No!*

This time he would suffer through whatever awaited him here at the end of time, and he would face it without the glasses.

Kevin closed his eyes and lay like that, in the midst of the sickness, barely able to think or move, until, in the timeless silence, he heard someone knocking on a door.

Kevin thought it was some sort of hallucination. His droopy eyelids lifted part way, and he waited until he heard it again. *Knock-knock-knock!* It came from somewhere inside his house.

Kevin hauled himself out of his bed and into the hallway of many doors. *Knock-knock-knock!*

It came from the second door to the right—a heavy whitewashed oak door that rattled each time it was rapped upon.

Kevin had sparked out quite a few entrances to many places, and he had no idea where this particular door led.

*Knock-knock-knock!*

If Kevin was the last soul on earth, then who

was knocking on the door? The terror of the thought did battle with Kevin's curiosity.

*Knock-knock-knock!*

His curiosity won. Kevin grabbed the brass knob and turned until the mechanism clicked.

A breeze pushed its way through as the door opened, smelling sweetly of spring grass and trees. A man stood at the threshold. He was lean and good-looking, with a face not unlike Kevin's father's, only younger—he was twenty-three or twenty-four at the most. He wore a bathrobe.

Kevin thought he knew who this was, although he never expected Him to look like this. Under normal circumstances, Kevin would have felt awe and amazement—but then, under normal circumstances, he wouldn't have come face to face with God in a bathrobe. Now, as things stood, Kevin was simply too sick and too exhausted to feel anything at all.

The visitor at his threshold, on the other hand, seemed awed enough for both of them. He looked around at the walls and at the hole where the bathroom had been with childlike wonder. "Wow," he said.

"I'm sorry," said Kevin. "I'm sorry I screwed up so bad."

"You look like crap," said his guest. "You should be in bed." Then he took Kevin in his arms and brought him back to his bedroom, where he laid Kevin down and covered him with a blanket.

The man introduced himself as "Brian," and said he had come a long way.

"I'm sorry," croaked Kevin again.

"Save it," said Brian. He went to wet a towel and then used it to blot Kevin's head. "You'll be sick for a while," said Brian. "It'll get worse before it gets better, but I'll stay here with you."

"I'm sorry for what I did," begged Kevin.

"Just shut up and get some rest."

Kevin drifted in and out of consciousness as the sickness got worse, but Brian never left his side. Kevin thought he would die a thousand times over, but after what seemed like an eternity, it began to get a little bit better, as Brian had promised.

Kevin opened his eyes to find Brian sitting at his desk, building an elaborate Lego castle.

"Amazing things," said Brian. "I haven't played with these in years."

"What time is it?" asked Kevin.

"Nine-forty-two."

"Oh, right," said Kevin. "Duh!"

Brian sighed. "I'd better get back." He got up from Kevin's desk. "It's been surreal, but I've got places to go and people to see."

He took one last look around and laughed. "What a scream," he said. "I hope I remember this."

Kevin followed him to the hallway, his legs feeling stronger by the minute.

"Wait, you're just gonna leave me here?"

"That's the general idea."

"But you can't go!" cried Kevin. "Everything's still screwed up—and what about the glasses?"

"The glasses!" said Brian with an amazed grin, as if remembering something he had completely forgotten.

"I can't get myself out of this," said Kevin. "Even if I had the glasses, I can't undo the things I've done—I've tried every which way. . . ."

Brian shrugged. "Did you let someone else try? Maybe someone else could use the glasses to fix the things you can't."

The thought robbed the very air from Kevin's lungs, making him dizzy and speechless. As he thought about it, Kevin realized that Brian had the answer. How selfish and short-sighted Kevin had been! Why couldn't he have seen that it would take someone else to "re-imagine" the mess he created? Teri, Josh—anybody could have done it if Kevin had let them try. It had always been in his power to fix things—by the simple act of letting it be in someone else's power. But there were not others left—only Kevin and Brian.

Brian grabbed the doorknob.

"Wait," said Kevin. "I've got an idea. The glasses are probably healed by now. I'll go get them and give them to you—and *you* can fix everything!"

"That's the whole point," said Brian. "I *can't* fix things."

"Yeah, you can," pleaded Kevin. "You can fix anything—I'll bet you don't even need those dumb old glasses to do it, either."

Brian just shook his head. "What are you, nuts? Who do you think I am?"

"I *know* who you are," said Kevin, in a solemn voice reserved for extremely important information.

"No," said Brian. "I think you're still seriously clueless. Take a good look, Shrimpoid." Then Brian knelt down to Kevin's level and looked into Kevin's eyes—eyes the same shade of blue as his own. This close, Kevin's blurry vision came into focus, and he could see everything about Brian's face that he had missed before; the slope of his nose and the shape of his eyes, and the tint of his dirty-blond curly hair. It was all so very familiar—so familiar that for the strangest moment, Kevin thought he was looking into a mirror.

Brian didn't have to tell him who he was, because now Kevin knew. He should have known from the very beginning—not because of the hair, or the eyes, or the tone of his voice, but because his visitor chose to call himself Brian, which was, after all, Kevin's middle name.

"But, how . . . ?"

"Beats me," said "Brian." "Maybe you asked to see your own future while those supercharged shades were still on your face. So, do you like what you see?"

Kevin smiled. "I like it a lot." Kevin was about

to begin throwing out all the questions—what do I grow up to be? Where do I live? What happens to everyone else? But before he could say another word, a sound came wailing in from beyond the door. It was a very familiar drone, and now Kevin knew how Brian's journey was possible. The sound on the other side of the door was an alarm clock.

"Gotta go." Brian pulled open the door. "Can't sleep my life away!"

"But how do I get out of this?" asked Kevin.

"I can't remember."

As Brian crossed the threshold, Kevin peered in, but Brian stepped in his way, blocking his view.

"No peeking," he said.

"Right. See you later, Shrimpoid."

"Who are you calling Shrimpoid?" said Brian with a smile, and Kevin noticed for the first time that "Brian" was about six feet tall.

Brian closed the door, slicing off the sound of the alarm, and when the echo of the door had faded, the stillness of 9:42 returned once more.

Kevin, still weak and a little tipsy, hurried downstairs, out the back door, and up the hill. He hadn't seen much of the world beyond "Brian's" door, but the glimpse he did get was enough. He saw a life for himself! A world with a blue sky and trees and sunshine. There *was* a way out!

At the top of the hill, the glasses were nowhere to be seen.

Kevin carefully searched through the dirt beneath the twisted tower, in an ever-widening circle, with patience and determination. Finding a needle in a haystack was, after all, a simple enough thing if one took the time to do the job right.

Kevin found the glasses in the tall grass near one of the legs of the tower. Sure enough, the glasses had pulled themselves back into one piece, and although the lenses were still covered with hairline fractures, they were already beginning to disappear, one by one.

*The glasses will always be here,* thought Kevin. They would always be there, waiting—but they weren't necessarily waiting for him, were they? That was just in his own head. The glasses, after all, were just a machine. Kevin's putting the glasses on was no different than if he had gotten behind the wheel of a monster truck and headed downtown. If he ended up totaling every car in town, it wouldn't be the truck's fault—he had no business driving the thing to begin with.

With that in mind, Kevin slipped the shades into his pocket and decided to go looking for a truck driver.

Just a few miles north of town, Kevin hit the front of the storm, where stationery raindrops hung in the air like an impossibly dense fog, soaking him to the bone. As he walked along the highway, he noticed that things around him were changing. It wasn't just his eyes, he was certain of it. The buildings and trees around him were only shadows, and even the raindrops that hung in the air seemed less and less real.

It was as if now that the world had stopped, it was beginning to fade away like an old snapshot. Soon it would all disappear into gray nothingness.

Kevin trod the wet roads, resting only when he absolutely had to, on a trek that would have taken many days had clocks been counting time.

Kevin trudged through cities, then towns, then into wilderness, until he finally came face-to-face with the mountain.

The Divine Watch, robbed of its color, disappeared into the rain clouds. Kevin forged his way to the base of the mountain, resting for only a few moments before beginning the climb.

He made his way up and up until the clouds became a thick mist around him. Then they gave way to a sky the likes of which had never been seen before. Though it was already beginning to fade, the sky of Kevin's imagination was magnificent.

It looked like a painting in brilliant shades of blue, violet, and red. Spheres of planets loomed huge and imposing on the horizon, beneath triple suns that cast Kevin's shadow in three different directions. It was every bit as impressive as another world could be, but now that he had seen it once, Kevin didn't care to see it again. He would just as soon cram it all back into his own head and forget about it.

The earth below had disappeared beneath end-less layers of clouds. All that remained were the sky and the mountain.

Kevin climbed hand over hand in a constant rhythm toward the heavens until, at last, his hand came to rest atop the Divine Watch. He pulled himself up to see the empty tabletop of smooth granite. Then he pulled the glasses from his pocket.

Yes, thought Kevin, they would always be here, never too far out of reach—but that was okay. He had the power to resist—he just needed to remember that.

Kevin opened the glasses and set them on the flat surface of the Divine Watch.

"Here," he said to the top of the mountain. "These look better on you."

Kevin waited and watched.

At first nothing happened, and he thought with a horrible sinking sensation that he had failed. Then Kevin noticed it; the three shadows of his hand began to move.

Up above, the suns converged into a single sun, and the planets slowly slipped off the horizon.

A breeze became a wind and the wind became a gale that whipped across Kevin's face, and as Kevin stared into the glasses, he saw, for the first time, what Josh had always seen. Beneath the swimming colors on the surface of the glasses was an eternity—an unknowable depth. Dimensions

and universes—*possibilities*—so many of them
that Kevin had to look away for fear that if he kept
staring into the mind behind the glasses now, he
would be dragged down into it and disappear.

Everything happened more quickly now. The
clouds below him boiled. Night became day, day
became night, over and over again, and Kevin's
mind began to swirl, all his facts and fictions
becoming one big blur as reality was once more
re-imagined.

There was a moment—just an instant in time—
when reality and dreams met each other before
switching places. It was a moment of absolute in-
sanity, when Kevin couldn't tell the difference between what existed and what did not and couldn't
make sense of his broken thoughts. Where was he?
What was going on? Then the moment passed, and
when it did, the suns, the planets, and the rain-
storm fell deep into the core of Kevin's mind,
where they, once and forever, ceased to exist.

Kevin thrust his hand up through the wind, desperately trying to grasp something, as his mind
took hold and he remembered where he was and
what he was doing.

He was climbing a mountain.

With eyes wet and cold, Kevin reached out his
right hand, and finally his fingertips touched the
flat top of the Divine Watch.

"What's it like, Kevin?" Josh yelled over the
wind.

"Do you see anything up there?" called Hal.

"Well, what's happening up there, Midas?" yelled Bertram. "We ain't got all day!"

There *was* something there! Kevin pulled himself up another inch until his head eclipsed the rising sun, and the object was trapped in his shadow.

"Its . . . it's a pair of glasses!" said Kevin.

As Kevin stretched out his arm toward the sunglasses, the wind screamed in his ears, and reality suddenly took hold.

What was he doing here? He could fall! He could die! What was he thinking! Panic screamed at him like a thousand voices in the wind, demanding he leave this dangerous place now and get back to the campsite this very instant.

He drew back his hand, leaving the glasses untouched and undisturbed.

"Let us get up there, Midas. Get out of the way!" demanded Bertram.

Kevin tried to make room for the others, but he moved too quickly and lost his balance.

Kevin fell onto Josh, who toppled onto Hal, who crashed into Bertram, and the foursome plunged down the rocky cliff, rolling over sharp rocks and over each other until they smashed against a hard plateau fifty feet below.

Everyone wound up with minor cuts and bruises except for Kevin.

Kevin broke his leg.

# CHAPTER 17

## After the Fall

"It'll be okay," said Bertram. "I'll go get help," Bertram turned to go, but before he did, he punched Hal in the arm. "This is *your* fault," he said.

Hal ran off to search for branches to help make a splint, and Josh sat beside Kevin, propping him up and helping him bear the pain.

The break was bad. Kevin had always imagined that if he broke his leg, he would die from the pain, but he didn't.

"Does it hurt real bad?" Josh asked Kevin.

"Real bad," answered Kevin. "But not real, *real* bad."

"You'll be fine, Kevin, don't worry," said Josh.

The sun was higher now, filling the valley with a warm glow. The light hit Kevin's face, and he relaxed just enough for the pain to drop a notch.

There was something gnawing at Kevin's

mind—as if there was something he ought to remember, but it was slipping away. All that remained was a certainty that he would be okay— that Bertram would bring help, that his leg would heal, and that the world would go on. Even something as unpredictable as falling and breaking his leg did have a very predictable outcome—and that simple thought comforted his piercing pain. On its worst days, the world still made some sort of sense, and that was a good thing.

"Look, Josh," said Kevin, peering down at the spectacular view in the valley before them. "Way down there—I can see cars at that picture spot we stopped at. The people look like ants!"

"How can you see that?" asked Josh. "You're blind as a bat without your glasses."

*Glasses?* thought Kevin. *Do I wear glasses?* He was baffled for a moment, but the moment passed. "I have twenty-twenty vision—you know that, Josh," said Kevin. "I don't wear glasses."

"That's right," said Josh, scratching his head. "That's funny . . . I wonder why I thought you did. . . ."

Beneath them, the morning unfolded on the valley in glowing shades of green and gold. A lazy smile stretched across Kevin's face.

"Kevin," asked Josh, beginning to worry, "you okay?"

"Never better," said Kevin, and he laughed, because he knew it was true.

Josh tried to hold back a smile but couldn't. "You're crazy, Kevin," said Josh. "Certifiable," but they both laughed long and loud until their voices rang out across the valley, echoing from here till doomsday.